Strangers in love

Jamie Neve

Enjoy!

Neve

Aug 2026

Text copyright © 2019 Jamie Neve

All rights reserved

This book is dedicated to Truman, Holly and 'Fred'.

And to Kassa Coffee, St Leonards on Sea, England where the initial manuscript was written.

One

I first saw Gloria seconds after she landed a swung right fist into Tommy Belotti's lips in Spring 1944 in an alley in downtown Queens. She was five years old. He had called her names I heard the neighbors' pa use for his daughter when she came home so late it was early morned. But she was nineteen. Tommy ran home, cried loud to his mom. She went around to Mrs Raccio's, Gloria's ma, gave her a piece of her mind. Mrs Raccio gave Mrs Belotti a piece of her left fist, took out a tooth. You didn't argue with Gloria and her ma.

As I traipsed behind Mrs Belotti, along with six or seven other kids who had gone along for the entertainment, I decided I was in love with Gloria. My taste in women was always questionable.

'No, I don't remember you. You sure we were in the same class? Mrs Rimmer's? But I weren't in school often, I don't recall many kids there.'

Gloria, now aged twenty-one, stood with one stiletto heel on the bottom stair of the apartment block where I, and now she, lived. Down Brooklyn way, not the worst, not the best neighborhood. Gloria had gone up in the cosmos of New York.

'Roy. Roy Dalton. My father owned a deli on Queens Boulevard. I had a sister, Evelyn, two years ahead of us, you stamped her foot after she accidentally knocked your ice cream outta your hand in the summer of '45.'

'Gee, you want me to remember that? I stamped on a lot of kids back then, still do. But not kids now, you know.'

Gloria, at eight in the morning, wore a red swing dress topped with a similar colored coat. Her brown waved hair hung to sweep her collar, styled in fashion to match the front cover of *LIFE* magazine. Her makeup, strong like a castle's fortifications, layered red and black around lips and eyes respective. Gloria's lips fascinated me. My sister said they were called 'cherub-shaped'; full and lush of skin, just waiting to be sucked and eaten slow. Her eyes, war-painted, reminded me of old photos I'd seen of an actress, Jean Harlow. I read she had died young.

'No, sorry, I was just hoping to jog your memory. But you recall the Berlotti boy? You thumped him near every month, he kept shouting names at you.'

Gloria shifted her position on the stairs. Nylon grazed nylon; her legs, shaped long and well defined despite her short height of around five three, switched places. The clutch bag, blushed a fainter red than her outfit, dangled loose from her elbow. She hitched it back up her arm.

'Him I know. He's dead now, you know? Got filled with lead over in Queens two years ago, he'd tried to cross Cigar Charlie. Bad choice. Don't you ever do that, Ray.'

'Roy.'

'Yeah, Roy. Don't do that, not less you got things on the guy kept safe and secret with a lawyer.'

I had heard of Charlie. Everyone had in the neighborhoods around here. He controlled everything illegal, and most legal too, and he left you alone, if you left him and his cronies alone. You had to be brave or foolish to try to take his businesses down. You had to be Robert Olsen, connected to a rival gang and now gone honest as a PI, to risk that.

'I appreciate the words, Gloria. So, you just moved in here?'

Gloria hesitated. Changes of conversation threw her. Sharp as a new-ground, razor-edged knife one moment, she could go blunt and near comatose the next. She ran a hand up over her hair, checked every wave held firm and perfect.

'Yeah, day or two ago, but I ain't been here yet, been out working, you know. Friend of mine owns the apartment, gonna let me sleep here whenever I want.'

'Cool. I'm down here, number three, been here a year, got a job at Johnson and Cohen, lawyers on 4th.'

Gloria's eyebrows showed interest in my comment, her eyes seemed fixed on something else far away.

'Lawyer? You might be useful, if I ever face the chair. Hah.'

Gloria's laugh was edged with the sound of a thousand Lucky Strikes smoked. It was the sexiest sound I had ever heard. Next to her voice.

'And why would you get there? You're too clever to get caught for anything.'

Gloria's smile lingered. I wished I could keep it there forever.

'No one escapes too long. Even Charlie will get there, or inside Sing Sing, sometime. You stay clear of trouble.'

I needed to leave, get into the office before Mr Johnson called out for his first coffee of the day. But I wanted to stand here, talk with Gloria until the sun drowned behind a new-erected skyscraper.

'So, you working around here?'

Gloria edged one stair higher, a step nearer a bed longed for since early last night I wagered. Her eyelids batted slow, the warmth of the block's foyer seeped through her tough Apple skin, lulled her brain into a Lethe-type stupor.

'Kinda bit of everything, dealing cards for guys with too much moolah to waste, pouring drinks for folks already leaking alcohol through their ears.'

'That's almost poetical, Gloria. I don't remember you writing lyrical in Miss Heimer's lessons.'

'Huh, I guess I must be mixing with a few well-educated guys these days. Most can't say more than one word.'

Gloria swayed, put a hand out onto the white-glossed banister, steadied herself and gazed somewhere over my head. I shook my watch into view, reckoned I could make it on time if I left now.

'I gotta go earn dimes, Gloria. See you around if you're staying here a while.'

'Oh yeah, sure, I'll be in the apartment a few weeks at least. If you see a tall guy come out of there, don't talk to him or get in his way. He ain't nice most of the day.'

I swallowed, cleared my throat.

'I'll keep away from him. He's not causing you trouble, is he?'

'Me? No, he keeps me safe. Or so he says.'

Gloria turned away, the last phrase faded into the air, her feet dragged heavy up a stair or two. She swiveled around. My eyes still rested on her figure.

'Good to see you, Roy. There, I got it right that time, didn't I? Not such a fat-head, am I?'

'No, you certainly aren't that.'

Gloria missed the longing in my tone. She wouldn't have been looking for it in the first place.

Two

I sipped the whiskey, let it run around my mouth before spiraling down my throat like a vanquished ship lost in the whirlpools of Charybdis. Bars were not the usual place to ease my tiredness, not on a Thursday evening with work the next day and files to be made neat and complete by the weekend break. Maybe I was hoped I would return to my apartment just as Gloria left for her club or bar. Maybe I wanted to run her around my head in a busy environment. Not the lonely four walls of a single man's rooms.

Gloria had gone up in the world. If she could afford to stay in an apartment block where most people went to work in smart suits and with leather cases held confident. My ma and pa subsidized me. I guess this tall guy did likewise for Gloria. Or whoever paid the man his dollars. When Gloria laid out the Berlotti boy her father had been gone twelve months at least, run off with a broad who took her store's cash with her as an unofficial gold watch. Gloria's ma had welcomed a thin Winston chain-smoked short guy with hair curled tighter than Shirley Temple by the end of the week. He didn't hide his nasty side outside the apartment; twice he threw knives at me and my friends when our football spun too long for Dipper, our wide receiver who lacked pace and catching ability, and the ball landed loud against the Raccio window. Gloria got out the house soon she could, when she was ten in human years, twenty-five in New York ghetto years. Rumor was the new man had hit hard when she tried on her ma's lipstick; a few voiced quiet he'd tried to put hands where they shouldn't go on such a young body. Either way she was best out of that apartment. She was took in by an aunt four streets away, the authorities turned a blind eye or didn't want the publicity of underage scandals, and Gloria began to turn up regular at classes. And I got to stare at the back of her Aphrodite-sculptured head for two years.

Some guys prefer legs, others breasts, or asses, or lips or eyes. Me? The back of Gloria Raccio's head held me fixated. It was the way her brown hair laid in layers over her head, waved down to rest, in those times, with a ruffle of curls across her shoulders. Every minute or two her right hand would rise up, stroke back a strand which had declared independence of the chosen style, tried to float away free, been apprehended on the run. Gloria's fingers, like her legs, surprisingly long for a shorter woman, would hook up the errant hair, twist it in punishment, place it precise back where it had dared to move from. As she did so, her cheek and eye would come into my view. And my heart would skip a beat, my handwriting judder unneat on the page.

The only time of day which matched these wonderful minutes was when Gloria deigned to join in our football scrambles out of class. No other girl was allowed near our patch of the concrete yard out the back of the school where Super Bowls were run regular two or three times a week. She could catch a fly flown fast across the classroom and had an elbow so sharp no boy ever tried to tackle her, even though many wanted to feel her body, even prepubescent, against their testosterone-swelling skin. Hire her for a dollar to run a pattern or two for your team, you were certain to carry off the trophy hasty made out of cardboard and illicit-used yellow paint from the locked art cupboard. Yeah, it would be Gloria who picked the lock with a hairpin and a lick of her cherub-shaped lips. To watch that tongue caress that thin unbent strip of metal gave me the earliest indication of the heights a woman could take a man. I spent the first ten minutes of the football games with my legs crossed.

Gloria faded out of horizons when she left class one Friday afternoon in eighth grade never to be seen again within the corridors of academia. I studied hard, went to college, now law school and a legal firm. My only sightings of the brunette descended from the wrong end of Olympus were glimpses on the street of a fast-paced woman clad in fashions seen last on neon billboards or rushed-flushed along sidewalks with a brown leather shoulder bag almost certain stuffed with rolls of dollars collected from frightened store owners or landlords with extorted renters. Either encounters saw

Gloria fly-by with no glance or nod for an alumnus of her irregular chalkboard days.

Now she laid her body down one flight of stairs above me. The gods work in mysterious ways. Or they taunt the good and law-abiding with an angel tinged with blackened wings.

Three days later I'd seen no more of Gloria. With thirty minutes to kill before a drink with fellow lawyer-in-training Eddie Mills I wandered up the stairs to the upper story of apartments in our block. I knew Mrs Stinson who lived one door on from Gloria. She often left her place open in the hope of a gossip or twenty with anyone on their way out or in.

'Roy, not seen you for a while. What you doing up here?'

'I was just wandering, Judy, thought I better show myself to you else you might call the cops out to come look for me.'

'Haven't seen a donut boy this way for many a month, we attract nice clientele now, on the whole.'

'That we do. And I hear we got a new girl next door to you.'

Judy rolled her eyes, folded arms across her light blue cardigan. Her hair, once natural red, now glowed with the false color of a downtown salon run by her cousin's son. The style recalled Lana Turner in the 1940s. For once a cigarette didn't stick to her lower lip, along with an ash column hung in a one-sided match with gravity.

'She's a sheba, Roy, a girl with sex appeal, nothing more. You stay away from her. I hear her language through the walls, even when she's alone she uses words only troopers would mutter in the war with all hell rung out around them. And her clothes...you'd think we were a Cigar Charlie or Sam Olsen club with private rooms out back.'

'She have many visitors then?'

I leaned against the door frame, tried to show indifference to the answer.

Judy coughed.

'Well, someone walks her home, let's just say that. Big guy, shoulders like a wrestler. But he don't have a hand or arm on her. Soon as she goes in, he leaves. But one weekend, a man in a suit stayed both days. I saw them out down the theater streets on the Saturday, arm in arm. Very suave he looked, but you wouldn't want your daughter bringing him home as son-in-law material.'

'Why not?'

'He had the look of a killer in his eyes. I seen them on *Perry Mason*, tell them a mile off. Hair greased, eyes evil, hands everywhere.'

I fought to hide the annoyance I felt, kept my face straight, my eyes undiminished. The news confirmed my own suspicions of Gloria's choice of employment. Even in class it was rumored she ran envelopes for the local gang affiliated to Cigar Charlie, the main gang boss around the block. She carried more dollars in her jeans' back pocket than any of us saw from our Saturday jobs throwing newspapers into the mailboxes of middle-class families. I spent ten minutes fending off inquiries into my own love life from Judy, walked downstairs with a heavy heart, slumped onto the sofa with Sinatra sung sad in the background.

Three

'Hey, Roy, what you doing here?'

The bar regulars turned to stare at the guy Gloria had welcomed with wild enthusiasm. I felt like turning and looking at myself. She'd remembered me, remembered my name. I flushed, shrugged shoulders like a regular bar hanger, sidled up the counter with my best James Dean swagger.

'Just passing, Gloria.'

I dropped in her name to reinforce the audience's opinion I was the long-lost love of this dreamy girl. Leaned against the teak counter, I dropped a bill casual on the top next to a couple of emptied, uncollected beer glasses. Gloria crossed over to opposite me. Her hair was up, her mascara light, her lips almost nude. She wore a check shirt in blue with turned up navy jeans. A white belt tugged tight around a waist I could probably put both hands on and touch fingers together. She looked at me like I was family.

'What poison can I get you?'

The words smoked out from those cherub lips like a potion ushered from a mischievous nymph's mouth. Her fingers splayed over the counter, beat a tune from a singer I didn't recognize, the painted red nails Morse-coding a message of love. Or so I fantasized.

'Whiskey.'

'Didn't have you for a whiskey guy.'

Gloria's fingers moved over a glass and rack-hung bottle like a team of gunners locking and loading a howitzer.

'I'm usually a beer man. Just sounded weak in this bar where everyone has a small glass in front of them.'

Gloria leaned forward over the counter, pushed my drink slow toward me, a conspiratorial look on her face.

'But they're all losers, sad, lonely, wives left at home with bawling kids, or nothing but the radio to love them late into the night.'

'And me? You think I got a happy wife at home?'

11

'If you had a happy wife, you'd have her hand in hand here with you, and you'd be drinking your beer long and warm.'

'So then I'd be one of the sad, lonely guys?'

Gloria stepped back, childish laughter played quiet on her lips, spread wide on her face.

'You're twisting my words, Roy. You just not met the right woman yet, you ain't one of the sad ones. You got a good job, prospects, you'll soon be living in some detached house way out from the noise and dirt of these streets. You'll not even remember me.'

I picked up my whiskey, sipped quick, grimaced at the rare rough taste that hit my throat.

'I don't think I'll ever forget someone like you.'

I looked Gloria straight, hoped she might read the genuine affection stamped there. But her thoughts were cut off by the main door swung back hard.

'Eh, Gloria, not seen you working this bar for a while. Come here.'

A burly, fifty-something man walked in with arms spread wide. His dark overcoat hung open, underneath displayed an expensive striped suit cut perfect by a tailor paid by the hour. A trilby hat sat firm back on his head. His face suggested time spent on islands where the sun had no tall buildings to compete with and where everyone strolled hot sand in the latest Jantzen swimwear.

'Archie! Oh my, you look the bee's knees. Love the coat.'

Gloria flipped up the counter flap, ran on stilettoed heels to the new guy, and hung like a puppy dog pulled tight on a toy around his thick neck. Her lips smacked a kiss on his own, crushing in the process the mustache grown to outline his mouth in imitation of a Mexican bandito. His hands wrapped large on her waist, held her in place, while he stared into her sparkled eyes.

'Gloria, it's so good to see you. You should have come with us, I would've died to see you on the beach in very little.'

Gloria banged a finger on the guy's nose.

12

'Now, now, Archie. Maureen wouldn't have liked that.'

'You know what Maureen can do. Your body is a match for any Hollywood gal, and I wanna see it spread over warm sand in a tight-materialed swimsuit.'

'Archie, there are gentlemen in this establishment, you can't put pictures like that inside their minds, they'll run off home hot and bothered.'

The guy named Archie let Gloria down slow onto the floor. His hands felt a line over her body from waist to shoulder. Splayed fingers remained rested on her collarbone.

'Hey, I pay for you to work these joints, Charlie doesn't buy you your clothes, your shoes, your hair. I do. He gets a good return from guys who spend heavy in here and in the back rooms flick-flapping losing cards. I'd like something in return too. Apart from the chance to run eyes over you in a crowded bar.'

I drank deeper from my glass, struggled to hide my distaste of the liquor and the conversation played out in front of an audience of envious men. Maybe it was time to leave, go find my usual bar, one frequented by would-be lawyers, bank managers, and business guys with no time to take their eyes off the ball headed toward financial security and retirement on the golf course.

Gloria unhooked herself, grasped Archie's hand and dragged him to the counter.

'What'll you have? Bourbon?'

'In here? Give me the best you got, I'll try not to spit it on the sidewalk.'

'Archie. You'll put off my customers. Ray here's an old friend of mine, you don't want him deserting to a bar belonged to Old Slab Sides Sam, do you?'

I looked over, tried to sound cool and city-worn.

'Roy. It's Roy.'

Gloria flapped a hand my way.

'What? Oh, yeah, Roy.'

I smiled at Archie. He didn't notice it, or me, stared straight over my head. His drink dropped in front of him. No dollars changed hands. Gloria leaned over the counter, her blouse with one button extra loosened, the flesh of her cleavage poked pink toward her benefactor.

'Now, Archie, why you back in town then? You got business. Or trouble?'

'Neither's going to be talked about here. I came in to see you, tell you to put your best dress on tonight, I'll pick you up around ten, gonna be a long night over at Dino's.'

'Oh, just like that. You walk in, change my life, walk out.'

'That's what I did two months ago, didn't I? I don't see you complaining about it.'

Gloria inched back across the teak surface, a slice of pleasure removed from her face.

'I would've liked notice, Archie. I got a life too.'

The guy reached out, placed a hand over Gloria's forearm, the grip firm. Firm enough for me to see Gloria wince behind the fixed smile.

'Your life is mine while I pay your way. Folks are expecting you tonight, no one floats around the card table better than you, the guys empty their billfolds fast, write out IOUs they can't deliver, and are stacked neat inside my pocket for future plans. And you'll get a new wardrobe or two out of it.'

Gloria lost the smile, pouted, nodded her head side to side, looked away from Archie, caught my eye. Did she want me to sail in and whisk her away, pressganged to another shoreline? She looked away, returned to the big guy with the strong hand.

'A whole new wardrobe of clothes?'

'A whole one.'

'What time you pick me up?'

'I'll send Lorenzo around, say quarter to ten, he knows you always run late painting yourself pretty.'

Archie released his grip, reached over, kissed Gloria on the cheek. She didn't shun away but didn't return the parting embrace. Her eyes, I judged, kept focused on the clothes she might rack up row on row in the wardrobe.

The door closed behind the departed Archie. I edged along the counter, nearer to Gloria, fingered my glass, now half empty.

'You made some interesting friends since we ran the schoolyard.'

Gloria picked up a washed glass from behind her, began to wipe it with a cloth printed blue and white in a striped pattern.

'A business acquaintance. Isn't that what you guys would call him? Don't ever step across his path, he smiles mean, you don't wanna see him smile angry.'

'Good work, the poker games?'

'Your ears are too big, Roy. That right, it is Roy? Yeah, got it now. The games run late, right through to the early morning, I seen too many suns come up over New York. But, yeah, I get good tips, from the winners. And Archie's generous when he remembers.'

'You deal the cards, give out the drinks?'

'Me, a dealer? No. I walk the tables, lay hands on shoulders, encourage big bets, talk to the suckers stood at the bar waiting for an empty chair at a game.'

'Sounds a tiring occupation, couldn't you get work in a store, or a bookshop?'

Gloria stopped running the cloth around the inside of the glass with two fingers, a motion I had been slowly hypnotized by.

'Me? Stacking tins and cartons? At the games I get to wear heels and tight, sparkled dresses, shiny earrings and bright lipstick. It's glamorous!'

I sensed Gloria sold me the job as she sold the empty chair to the guy with the over-stacked billfold. Her smile came and went as her sentences began and ended. She finished off the glass, placed it with precision in a row of unused others. Fingers nudged it into a final position measured in tenths of an inch. The same fingers then stroked through her hair, patted a stray wave back into its preordained layer, then touched the edge of her mouth. Her eyes fixed somewhere halfway up the room between the door and the counter. Maybe she calculated how much it would cost to walk out and never come back. The cost not just in dollars. I guessed Archie wouldn't like to lose staff without a one-sided argument.

I swallowed a further quarter of my whiskey, left enough to stay a while longer. Whiskey was not my drink, two or three and I would start to say things I shouldn't. The last thing I wanted was to tell Gloria how I felt about her, have her laugh, put it down to the alcohol, and never look serious at me again.

'How'd you get into this work, not exactly timetabled on the careers' noticeboard.'

'Huh, you leave school early like I did, try to find work. You only get the ones where you show legs and smiles, if you're a woman. I done well to get into the card games.'

'That how you met this guy, this Archie?'

'Him? In a way, he played in a couple of games I worked at, he took me out for a meal after the second time, offered me a chance at his own tables. More money, better dresses. Couldn't say no.'

'And that's all you do? Walk the tables, pour a drink or two?'

'My, you are the newspaper man, aren't you? You got a side-line working for the *New York Times*?'

'Just curious, how life falls for people.'

'Well, you make sure you don't fall anywhere, it's sure hard to keep picking yourself up from the sidewalk.'

'What's the name of this place you go for poker?'

'You aren't gonna go waste your time and dollars there? You'll need your month's pay just to get entry to a game.'

'Not to play, watch the types who go, that's all.'

Gloria stepped away, poured a whiskey from a bottle into the glass of someone who looked like they inhabited the bar counter more than their sofa. No money changed hands, another debt racked up on the invisible board hung above the bottles upended on the wall. Gloria returned opposite me. A simple movement which made me feel warm inside and hoped grew jealous glances from the guys sat lonely around the room.

'And to stare at the pretty chicks like me?'

The three quarters of a glass of whiskey unraveled my tongue.

'I'd only stare at you.'

Gloria flung her head back, laughed silent with a wide-open mouth, showed off teeth straight and white like her ma's, another natural beauty inherited.

'Which creepy B movie you steal that line from? You the hard-drinking PI with a broad in every bar?'

I blushed. My words, rebounded off the sheen of Gloria's presence explained themselves inside my head, and I realized I put a toe too close to the partner I wanted to tango with.

'Sorry, the whiskey talked.'

Gloria leaned across the counter. A waft of perfume, one I had spent a Saturday afternoon being sprayed by young giggling assistants at a perfumery stand to find out it was Guerlain Shalimar, seduced the air around me. And her right hand came up to my cheek. Thumb and forefinger pinched firm on my skin. Gloria's face lingered inches from my own.

'The whiskey only speaks the truth hidden behind the fear of rejection.'

My mind whirled. At Gloria being so close, so desirous, and at the words she spoke. I struggled to focus eyes and thoughts.

'Where the heck did you get that from?'

My stupid question broke the moment. Gloria stood upright, the movement pulling her dress tight against her body.

'Some book I read, I guess. Or just watching guys sunk sad at these tables, then mumbling words as they're dragged outside.'

I swirled the last quarter of alcohol around its glass. My head still reran with the image of Gloria leaned so close and friendly.

'You read much? I don't recall you carrying books home from school.'

'School? Books about ma and pa with two smiling kids, and a dog, and a ranch or neat house with a drive and new automobile parked gleaming? Shucks, no, but a gun and knife adventure with a handsome hero with broad shoulders and square chin? Yeah.'

I swigged the whiskey, grimaced again at the taste, wondered if Mr Gleeson's expensive bottle in the office went down smoother with his Broadway clients, and pushed the glass away.

'Glad you read, maybe I can find something from my shelves, drop it off at your room.'

'I ain't gonna read about the laws of business.'

'Me neither, at home. My pa gave me all his Dashiell Hammetts, you might like to escape into them.'

'There's gotta be a love story in there, I wanna see a happy ending, or one I can cry over.'

'I'm sure I can find something.'

The door of the club opened, three guys and two women came in, their voices carried high into the room. They were followed by another two men. It seems the place was about to liven up. Gloria disappeared among the line of people firing out orders down the counter. Our cozy talk for two appeared to have a period punched hard into it. I looked at my watch, realized I needed to go tidy things up at home, finish a few pages of study for work. I drifted away, glanced back a couple of times, hoped to catch Gloria's eye to signal a farewell, but she was smiles and fluttered eyelashes with all the guys, in her element, in control, and in demand.

The fresh air outside slapped me awake. I breathed deep, picked up my spirits. I knew a little more about my former classroom partner; where she worked at other hours, what she read. Maybe in the morning I should go find a library book about poker.

Four

Two weeks and Gloria had become the proverbial passing ship in the night; clicked heels on the foyer floor, a door upstairs closed careless and loud, a curse uttered after the jangle of misfingered keys. Encounters on stairs seemed uncoordinated and off the script. I thought about a walk into the club where Gloria said she overlooked card games, but a combination of work demands and a hesitance to put myself too often in her eyeline kept me to bars where fellow untrained lawyers hung over counters to swap tales of low pay and mean-spirited bosses.

Then one rain-depressed evening saw me overcoated on a sidewalk with my feet following a brain's unannounced decision to lay eyes on the girl I couldn't get out of my head. I'd had to consult a map in the library to check the location of the club, it was off my known routes both in childhood and the present. I was surprised to find the neon sign winked bright not far from streets I did in fact know well. It stood alone in a narrow road, not planted ablaze like other such establishments in the hope of picking up strays from full-peopled tables or over-keen suits on doors. A taxi hummed with rear doors open opposite the single dark-glossed door. A man and a woman stepped out either side of the vehicle; his clothes sang of offices fifteen floors up with air conditioning, coffee bubbled on demand and a line of secretaries with fingers raised to tap out his every syllable; she swept toward the entrance in a fur-topped coat pinched tight at the waist, a clutch bag glittered in the neon reflection, a hair style so new it had yet to frontpage *Vogue* magazine. The couple walked in, the door held back for them by a suit who held a position in the shadowed porch to dissuade lesser mortals from venturing through portals to a dark destiny.

I walked past, reached the end of the street, crossed over to swing back along the sidewalk to the club. At the doorway I smiled at the guy who topped my height by six inches and my girth by double that.

'Free to come in?'

A head of hair lacquered by a product printed weekly in glossy magazines looked down at me. No smile broke back in recognition of my inquiry. Small lips moved small in the half light.

'Of course, sir. But it might cost more to leave.'

I narrowed my eyes. I kinda got what he meant, your billfold would be lighter by the time you trudged home, but I wasn't sure he quite got the right words in the right places to be enigmatic in his philosophical pronouncement.

'Sounds like my type of place, especially if it's got pretty chicks to pour the drinks.'

A hand spread wide on my shoulder, pressed tight.

'Keep your eyes on the cards, sir, anywhere else and you might be out here earlier than you guessed.'

I smiled again, this time with a nervous twitch in my cheek; the attempt to play the world-worn guy fallen flat at my shoes. The doorman opened the door, ushered me through with a sly smile.

Warm air cocooned my face, wall lights led me down a corridor, signs indicated restrooms, double doorways with heavy paneling gave way well-oiled to my touch. The room was near full; several tables populated to capacity with guys in various suits and jackets, dealers in tuxedos, four or five young women with trays of drinks meandered casual. A bar stood against the far wall, Gloria behind it alongside another woman. I walked along the outside of the tables where the lights cast shadows. A couple of guys lingered there. They might be players waited for a gap at a table or the management's sharp eyes in suits.

Time slipped by counted in rounds of hands. The choreographed dance of change a shuffle of chairs as the sensible ones left with loose dollars still held inside billfolds or grim-faced losers exited with stories half-concocted in muzzy heads to explain to the wife why she'd get less dollars to buy food this week. Gloria hadn't seen me, her eyes concentrated on guys with intent to play. Her hands purred down sleeves and backs, free drinks were caressed out, the reserve line to spare chairs kept shuffled forward. In return she accepted a wandered hand over her bare shoulders and rested too firm on hips covered by the light blue material of a close-fitted pencil dress sparkled with false diamonds. Gloria's hair looked new-styled, set and layered like a photographic model, her make-up bright with those cherub lips glossed to hypnotize the hesitant watcher.

A hand touched my arm. I jumped, wondered if the guy on the door had caught my eyes stared too long at Gloria.

'Hey, Roy, you're twitchy, you spotting cards for a friend? Or waiting for a girl to slip you something illegal for the weekend?'

Dan. Dan Whitney. A work colleague, a year older, ten in experience of the grubbier side of the city and its women. This would be the perfect location for him. If he had any moolah left in his billfold.

'No, no, just came along out of curiosity.'

Dan wore a dark brown suit, a work outfit, and carried a cream overcoat dangled from one arm. His hat perched back on his head, as usual, a tribute to his idol Sinatra. A Winston hung from the side of his mouth, half-dragged out.

'Curiosity? Dang that. Which chick you after? The blond over there? The black-haired one near the door?'

'No, Dan, neither. A neighbor of mine said she works here. I dropped by to see...'

'Her working conditions? Check out her rates of pay? Yeah, more like you're here to check out her outfit and the figure wrapped by it.'

Dan's elbow nudged me like a cliched act from a second-rate comedy movie. I knew my cheeks colored, I hoped the semi-darkness of the room's sidelines kept them gray to my friend.

'Forget it, we aren't all chasing everything in a skirt.'

'C'mon, which one is she? Promise I won't make a move on her. Less she's a real dreamboat.'

I knew it was pointless to mislead Dan, he would stay until he'd extracted the name, no matter how long it took.

'The one by the bar, just moved with that fat guy to the far table, brunette in light blue.'

I expected a fast retort, a remark so close to outright rude I would walk out or clip him with a fist. But silence replied. I turned to look at Dan, saw him staring stern, fingers on his cigarette, ash flared bright with his intake. He pulled the Winston out, blew a long stream of smoke into the room.

'You gotta be joking, Roy Dalton. Gloria? Gloria Raccio. You odd ball.'

'Why? You know her? Whaddya mean?'

Somehow I'd thought Gloria was my own little secret, apart from the guys and girls she worked with, someone I could admire, maybe grow close to, slow but sure. But if Dan Whitney knew her, half the city would.

'She's bad news, Roy. She runs with Cigar Charlie, heard it on the grapevine, seen it in bars. She collects money for him, rents paid high, protection rackets racked up higher. This work is like a day off to her.'

'And.., and.., where you seen her, apart from here? You sound like you work close to Charlie too.'

Cigar Charlie ran a criminal organization which controlled a large part of this area of New York. He vied with Sam Olsen, Old Slab Sides, for dominance. I wondered where Gloria's Archie sat in this web of dark intrigue.

'Ah, clubs here and there, and I know Micky Renson, over at Schwarz and Chubb, they deal with Charlie's problems, which quickly don't become problems for long, and I been with him when we seen Gloria pass over bags of moolah, and couple of times when she was out collecting. Hell, Roy, if she's your neighbor, move out fast.'

'People gotta earn a living however they can. Gloria's had a tough start in life.'

'Maybe, but they don't all sink down the sewer to find a life. You know her well?'

'Went to school with her, used to chase around in packs with her and her friends. She's not, not all, wrong, you know, not all bad.'

Dan punched me gentle on the arm. My cheeks still burned in the gloom. He leaned in close, noise in the room had risen as a guy threw down a winning hand, gathered in an untidy pile of chips.

'Don't let love blind you, broads like her will run you dry, use you, borrow dollars here and there, leave you the minute a better option arrives, usually with a thicker billfold and a faster car.'

'No, she's not like that, I...'

'They're all like that, Roy. Don't be a schmuck. Find yourself a girl like Barbara at the office, sweet, quiet, cuddly body, good housewife in the making. Move fast, I may take her down a drive-in soon if you don't.'

I snorted hard, pushed my hands into crumpled trouser pockets. My eyes fixed on Gloria. She smiled, fluttered eyelashes at a middle-aged suit fifty pounds overweight with a paunch which kept Gloria at a safe distance. She patted his arm, looked over to the bar from where another waitress had called her, left her guy and walked like a new-launched Hollywood star over to the counter. It wasn't just the suit's eyes and mine which followed her wiggling movement; half a dozen guys moved heads to track her short journey. A brief talk with the other woman, Gloria went behind the bar, fumbled below the counter. The door behind her opened. Dan shouldered me.

'Jeez, Roy, see what I mean?'

A man came through, tallish, in a dark blue overcoat, fedora hat laid lazy to one side, face flushed from a jog, probably along an alley behind the club. I looked over to Dan.

'Who is he then?'

'Detective Floyd Galvan.'

'Cops? Is this illegal here?'

'Crosses over many lines of law. But Galvan, so I've heard, also crosses those lines.'

The detective smiled as he approached Gloria, tucked an arm around her waist, drew her close, kissed her full and long on the lips. Dan gave me another nudge.

'Told you. She plays games for Charlie, and she's tucked up nice with the bad cops too.'

'Maybe she gives them information, maybe...'

'Grow up, Roy. She wouldn't meet him here to do that. Christ, you see that?'

I had. Gloria had withdrawn a roll of dollar bills, a thick roll, from her dress pocket. She planted it in the detective's hand, kissed him on the cheek, passed a glass of whiskey along the counter. They stood talking like old friends, hands on each other's arms, smiles given and taken. The money disappeared into the cop's jacket pocket as fast as he swigged down the drink, free it seemed. Gloria touched the man's arm again, turned away, gave her attention to a guy fresh stood at the counter.

Dan leaned in.

'Looks like they pay the cops to turn a blind eye to anything here that breaks the law. They're doing us out of profitable work in the courts.'

'Could be innocent. Gloria might be...might be buying a car from the guy, or...'

'Take those rose-tinted shades off, Roy. She must be deep in the mire here, she's the one trusted to pass over the moolah to the dodgy gumshoe.'

I stood, eyes gazed at Gloria. She played the hostess to perfection. But the woman who had stood at the bottom of the stairs, the little girl I remembered on the schoolyard. They were still there somewhere.

Five

Two days later I pushed open the door of Louis Chang's Laundry, a suit to be collected. Gloria sat in front of a twirling machine window, gum slow-chewed around her mouth. It was the first time I'd seen her since the poker club. The assistant at the far end raised a hand, went out back to find my item. I pulled a chair alongside Gloria. She still stared straight ahead. I stuck my legs out straight, one foot flopped over the over. A casual meet between friends, I hoped.

'Hey, you got free time to do all this? Thought you'd have a guy on call to do your washes.'

I smiled, hoped she would recall me, not think I was another john wanting to buy her drinks later that night.

'Hey, Roy.'

'You remember my name, guess my face can't be that ugly after all.'

'Stupid. You're cute. Go find yourself a pretty chick.'

'Maybe I will, when I'm earning decent money.'

'Dollars ain't everything, don't go chasing money to be happy.'

'You gone all philosophical again, Gloria. You writing poetry?'

'You and poems, what is it?'

'A song then. Put your thoughts down as lyrics. Can you hold a note?'

Gloria crossed her legs, showed off nylon-covered calves under a cream swing skirt. White pumps wrapped her feet, scuffed at the toes. A letter jacket, red and white, hung over a pink cardigan. She was a mix of college girl and housewife today.

'Long enough to drive you out the door.'

I smiled to myself, thought of something to say, anything to keep the conversation going, keep in the company of this beautiful woman. Gloria's eyes still followed the spins and swirls of clothes sud-soaked.

'Why the long face? You broke up with a guy? Lost your job?'

'Nada. Too many guys, too many jobs given me.'

'And that's a problem?'

'Yeah.'

A face I recalled seen as I left the club two days ago floated up into my memory.

'Not Olsen. Robert Olsen. I thought I saw him stood at the side of the room when I left...'

Gloria flashed a look at me. Just as I realized I'd let slip my visit to the club.

'You were there? You were at the game?'

I tried to grin, wasn't sure Gloria would take it the right way, let it slip into the ether unnoticed.

'You were there, Roy? Why? There are bad people around those games, you keep away.'

Genuine concern lay on her face. I wasn't sure if I should be pleased, that she seemed to care for me in a way, or whether I should be frightened by her worries.

'I was curious, happened to be out that way, met up with a colleague there.'

'Met up with a buddy? That's mighty strange, you happened to be in the same club as me. You got a passion for me or something?'

My mouth hung open, words tripped half-formed on my lips. What did I say? Yes, blurt out my love for her. Or deny it, destroy my real passion for this woman. I stuttered. Gloria's machine intervened, juddered loud, stopped its spin, lay ready to be emptied. She waved away the Chinese assistant, stood up, unpacked, piled high a plastic basket. I shifted my eyes toward the door, embarrassed in case I caught glimpses of underwear. Gloria placed everything into a dryer, fed the slot metal food, sat down back next to me.

'Olsen, me and Bobby, we been seeing each other a while.'

I was glad Gloria changed back to an earlier theme. To deny my devotion to her would hurt deep. Fear of rejection even more so.

'You and Olsen? I haven't seen him at the apartment block?'

'I stay at his place.'

'I thought this, this Archie was paying for your apartment?'

'Yeah, that's why I'm sat here dull and dumb. Too many guys.'

'So that's why I haven't seen you around the apartment? You been living with Robert Olsen?'

'Bobby. Yeah. We met at the theater...'

'Theater? You go to plays? Musicals? What?'

'No, I was there...on a work thing. I had to...escort a friend of Archie's, a business buddy of Charlie's. I bumped into Bobby.'

Gloria chuckled, the first brightness to spread over her face since I'd come in the laundry.

'He threw a drink over my dress. Huh, such a dumb ass. But he saved me from a fat guy with fat fingers that wandered loose and mean all over me.'

I wasn't sure I wanted to hear the rest, yet part of me wanted to know everything about Gloria's life.

'And you…?'

'Jeez, you want it kiss by kiss, Roy?'

'No, no, I just, I remember Olsen from law school. We were in the same class for three, four months.'

'He's a friend of yours?'

Gloria's question had an edge of sharpness hung about it. Was she worried Olsen and me might have met to discuss her? Was she concerned we might drink together later to swap stories?

'No, I hardly ever spoke to him. Another guy pointed him out to me, said there was a rumor Olsen was related to Sam Olsen. The gangster, you know?'

'Old Slab Sides Olsen? That gang boss? You kid me?'

'No, not at all. Apparently, Sam Olsen is known for, for chasing women. Story goes he's got several illegitimate kids around the city.'

'Huh, that would take the biscuit, wouldn't it? Me working for Charlie and slept close with a guy related to Old Slab Sides.'

I blanched embarrassed at her comment. Gloria looked at me, must have read my face.

'Sorry, Roy, I speak how things are, never been one to hide feelings, relationships, you know?'

'Sure, it's nothing, just getting my head around how you people live.'

'You people? You think I'm so different from you?'

Gloria had turned full face to me. Her cheeks were flushed red even over the rouge powdered there. Her eyes flared wide with something I read as anger or indignation.

'I'm sorry, Gloria, no, no, I didn't mean that, it's just, we guys in the office, it takes weeks to say hello to a doll, you flit one guy to another so quick...'

'Flit? What does that mean? You think I'm just a round heel girl? You think I do anything for dollars? That I chase any guy with a full billfold?'

Gloria's words and breath swept over me. The sweet aroma of her gum, now held balled inside her cheek, camouflaged the barbed words. My future hopes of getting to know this woman seemed shot to a thousand pieces. I dug fast to refill the hole I'd scooped out deep for myself.

'Please, don't misread me, Gloria, I didn't mean what you think, I...I...think a lot of you, really respect how you live your own life, aren't just circled up like so many of the chicks from school, a housewife with four walls and a kid for their whole world...'

Gloria's eyes pierced me hard. I'd never realized how fierce those brown pupils could be. I felt shredded. A naughty boy found out by a hard-assed mother.

'Why'd you keep talking to me, in the apartment, here, following me to the club? You some sort of weirdo, Roy? You got a girl, or you not got the spunk to put yourself out there?'

'Gloria. Please, calm down. I told you, we, we do things slower, the people I find myself working with, it doesn't look good if we rush around town, jump in and out of bed, it gets the firm a bad reputation, and...'

Gloria stood up, pulled her jacket straight, fastened it up. She strode to the door, pulled it open, looked back.

'Grow up, Roy, stop playing with those idiots you work for, live in the real, nasty, dirty world.'

With that as her exit line Gloria walked out. The door slammed shut behind her and put a period to our dialog.

'Your, your...'

My words bounced off the door's glass.

'...washing...'

An hour later I placed a neat bundle of dried clothes outside Gloria's apartment door. I hoped the laundry wouldn't miss one basket for a day.

Three hours on I studied a work document, rereading each line five times to remember what it said. The sound of paper on carpet switched my attention. Something white appeared under my door. I got up, walked over, glad to stretch my legs, picked it up, a torn off slip from a bar furniture order form. Scrawled large in blue-inked print read the words 'Sorry, life sucks some days, Gloria'.

For the first time since I left the laundry I relaxed. A bottle of wine stood on the table next my papers and books. I could take it upstairs, with two glasses, offer to drink to apologies. But, no, better not to chance my luck. I sat down, stroked away loose hair which had fallen across my forehead. The words on the documents in front of me began to make sense.

Six

Gloria came and went from her apartment upstairs in no coordinated order. For days she would be absent, then there overnight, then off again, back for a weekend, away for the next three days, and so on. I guessed her time was spent between Olsen, Archie and herself. More or less in that order.

We passed on stairs, on the concrete steps outside the apartment block, on the sidewalk early morned or late in the evening. We greeted, smiled, I touched my hat, she held a finger to her lips to signal no time for idle talk. Then, one Saturday night, as my fingers twisted a tie into shape for a visit to a movie with Dan and two women from our office, a door slammed up above. Followed by a chair pushed hard across bare wood flooring, a lamp tipped off a table, cutlery scattered into a sink, a coffee table upset with clinking glasses sent tumbled to the floor. I wondered if it was a tantrum or a deliberate cacophony of rage to bring interest from anyone nearby who had a soft spot for this brunette bombshell.

I stood outside Gloria's apartment, waited for a lull in noise, knocked four times with my knuckles.

'Gloria? You alright in there? You need anything?'

The door pulled back quick, stopped half open, a hand grasped tight around its edge. Gloria glared out at me; mascara smudged, scarlet lipstick blurred, one earring hung bent, hair fluffed and tossed loose in no style seen stared from out a salon's window.

'He threw me out, the rat threw me out, gone to walk in Hollywood with a platinum blond who acts like wet cardboard!'

I tried to process the diatribe. I had got as far judging whether it was Bobby Olsen or Archie who had broke up with her before Gloria's hand transferred from the door to my arm, pulled me inside, pushed me into an armchair reupholstered by her coat and red letter jacket.

'He fired a gun right next my head! Pulled the frigging trigger right by my ear! I thought I was a goner, gonna get my brains spattered over the pillow. You believe that? Put a gun to my head!'

My brain came up with Archie as the cowboy in this *High Noon* scene.

'Olsen, Olsen, the frigging PI, a guy who's meant to the good one, he tried to kill me. If he'd left a bullet in the chamber, I'd be naked in the morgue now! He ain't no good guy.'

Olsen? I reassessed the story line quick. Only one word came into my stewed head.

'Why?'

Gloria looked at me, eyes unblinked, hands placed on the waist of a dark green cocktail dress ruffled and out of line, something pulled on fast for an unexpected exit.

'Why? Why? He wants me a good girl waiting for him at home each day, then he's off chasing this little paper shaker with Monroe hair and breasts too darn big. Well, I ain't playing second fiddle to a chorus girl with a flat voice. I walked. The guy pulls a gun on me, I'm outta there.'

Gloria turned away, stumbled to the sofa, fell back over the arm rest, swung both legs up onto the cushions. Her dress fell away to show bare calves unwrapped by nylon. The volley of accusations had ceased. She stared at the ceiling, colored a smoked off-cream, seemed to draw inspiration from the sight, fumbled with a hand along the floor by the sofa, found an opened carton of Lucky Strikes. Fingers flicked a cigarette into her mouth. She stared around for a lighter or match. I saw a Zippo on a low table, went over, picked it up, thumbed it twice. A flame coughed into life. My hand shook as I lowered it close to the Lucky stuck on Gloria's lips. She dragged in deep, the end of the cigarette flared up bright.

Gloria laid back against the sofa armrest, picked the smoke out with slender fingers, exhaled a cloud around her head. My head wrestled with whether she played the Hollywood femme fatale or laid devastated for real, Olsen the one true love of her troubled life. She gazed up at me, lips now pursed.

'Thank you. You're my rock, you never change, you're always here. I need you, Roy, never move from here.'

I smiled small, wasn't sure what to say. Sat down again, the lighter placed on the table covered by newspapers strewn and jewelery thrown angry, I wondered what she wanted next.

'That where you been recent, Gloria? Over at Robert Olsen's?'

She inhaled again, let the intake circulate long around a body already too racked by nicotine and alcohol.

'Yeah. I moved in there, three days a week. I had to come here, keep Archie happy, not make him suspicious. And I got wardrobes in friends' places too, hard to keep track where my outfits are sometimes.'

'Archie was around here, a day ago, I passed him in the foyer.'

'Crap. That means he'll be back, I better not miss him again.'

I rubbed my fingers together, not sure if I should suggest something. Gloria eased up on the sofa, a stream of smoke drifted wavy from the cigarette's tip.

'Roy, stay here this evening, I'll cook something, cheer us up.'

Her words cut short my thoughts. To hear the word 'stay' seemed to drag out into the real world a half-lost dream in which Gloria and I lived happily ever after. The word 'cook' had me apprehensive.

'Sure, I can stay. Didn't realize you cooked?'

'Huh, I don't. But there's a first time, isn't there? Go look in the refrigerator, if it's as empty as my love life you might have to go shop us something.'

The machine in the kitchenette hummed with a smoker's rasp. Its inside was bare; milk too old, butter a brick, a piece of meatloaf dated early '50s I reckoned from its color. I closed the door.

'Maybe we should go find a diner?'

'No, I wanna stay in, I go out every day, to work here, there, all places. I want my own four walls tucked close around me.'

'Stay there, I'll go find something simple from the store around the corner.'

'Bring wine, Roy. Let's celebrate a life without Olsen and his endless whiskey.'

It took me quarter of an hour to pick vegetables and tins from shelves along with a bottle of something red with a name I recalled Dan using when we double-dated a pair of chicks the first day out of college. I peeled off bills, walked back fast to the apartment lest Gloria changed her mind or now laid on the sofa snored deep in Cinderella Land.

I opened her door, heard a drawer close.

'Hey, Roy, that was quick. Put everything on the table, I'll throw them in a pan, wish upon a star, see what comes out.'

Her voice sounded light, her spirit higher. I lowered the paper bag onto the small dining table bookended by chairs, started to unpack. Gloria walked through from the bedroom. She wore a light blue strapless bra and tap pants. Nothing else. I turned around fast, ran a hand through my hair, found the ingredients listed on a tin's side more fascinating than a new Cadillac. Gloria came over, stood next to me.

'So, what we got here, cook? Yeah, even I can do something with this, and it mightn't come with burnt edges.'

Her hand touched my back. She leaned forward, picked up another tin, glanced at the label, put it back down.

'Come help me in the kitchenette. I take it you can chop safe with a knife?'

Gloria was completely relaxed. She wasn't seducing me, teasing me, taunting me. Being in underwear in her own apartment was natural to her. And it was. It was just awkward for me, so close to a body wrapped thin in material pliant and sweet-smelling. Her bare midriff fascinated me whenever I glimpsed it in her movements around the small room. The skin smooth, tight, a mole to the left of her inverted tummy button. Pans rattled, taps creaked, pulsed out water in jets, knives clashed. And among it all was this angel-shaped creature, bare-footed, still make-up smudged, beautiful and vulnerable. Part of me hoped she would fall asleep after the meal so I could slip away to keep the memory unsullied by anything physically intimate and later regretted.

At Gloria's insistence we sat paired together on the sofa, plates on our knees, a fork gripped as a one-handed scoop. I concentrated hard to avoid food dropping on her legs or mine. Her bare thighs rubbed so close I could see the little goose bumps sat up alongside fine hairs. If a speck of tomato sauce had landed there, my heart would have cracked open had my finger had to rescue it from her skin.

Gloria ate fast, dribbled potato and sauce around her plate, wiped away drips from her lips with the back of her hand, talked non-stop of meals she'd made with a friend when lived poor first out of school and not yet entwined in Cigar Charlie's underworld.

Our shoulders grazed when she laughed out loud at a tale concluded about a guy kneed into submission on a sidewalk, her head lowered close to mine, her eyes and lips flashed, her breath, a mix of tomato, chicken, cigarette and perfume massaged over my face. I smiled back, forced a forkful of meat into my mouth before I sought to fill it with bee-stung lips.

'The wine, Roy! We forgot the frigging wine!'

The moment broke. I lurched back in the sofa seat as she rose up, put her plate on the coffee table, walked to the kitchenette. My eyes followed her slow-wiggled rear all the way. Heck, I was a guy, she was beautiful, in mind and very much in body. I shifted my look away, sat with fork half-lifted to remember I was sat in Gloria's apartment, sharing food, sat next to the girl in her underwear, as relaxed as lovers in their six months of commitment.

Gloria came back, two glasses pinched together in one hand, an opened bottle in the other. She bent down, placed the glasses on the table, put the wine next to them. Her cleavage showed clear in

34

my eyeline, small freckles painted pretty along the top of her bosom, the skin pale and white. Red liquid lapped to the top edges of the glasses as she poured out from the bottle.

'Let's drink to new loves, new lives, new frigging whatever.'

I laid a fork on my plate, picked up a wine. Gloria rattled hers against mine, sent drops of red liquid dripped down the glasses' sides, stared me straight in the eye, still bent down level with me.

'You're a brick, Roy. You saved my life tonight. I ain't gonna forget it.'

I sipped slow. Gloria swallowed long. I made a note in my head to pour the wine away during the refill. The last thing I wanted was to wake up tomorrow with Gloria dead-headed by alcohol and me listed in her head as just another guy who took drunk chicks to bed.

We ate and drank. Ate and drank. Talked about guys and girls ditched. Mainly Gloria about guys she'd loved, hated, kicked out. Or, reading between the curse-littered lines, the guys who had shown her the door. Though maybe not all at the point of a gun.

Plates scraped to the last line of sauce, glasses tipped up to the last clung dregs, we sat back, cushioned by cushions whose stuffing settled one way only, in a comfortable silence. Gloria's hand crept across the small space in between my legs and hers, let her fingers intertwine with mine. I was so sated both with food and drink it didn't even register as erotic or the foreplay to something where friends became lovers.

Gloria laid her head gentle on my shoulder.

'We ever spoke back at school, Roy? I don't recall we hung out in the same gang.'

'Nope. Raced around the schoolyard after you a few times. Couldn't catch you to kiss you though.'

'Always been a fast runner, saved me many a time, down an alley, along a sidewalk, inside a club.'

The comfort was gone to my head.

'Any time, Gloria, any time you wanna go out, wanna have a guy by your side, as a friend, just ask me.'

'Ah, that's cool, Roy. But I think you might want it go further some time. Unless you prefer the guys, of course, but I don't think you do.'

Her fingers squeezed mine. My heart leaped over the Moon, my cheeks felt warm-glowed even in the heat of the room. I forced myself to remember the evening had started with Gloria angered to tears over the end of one affair; now was not the time to suggest the launch of another.

I said nothing. And nothing whispered out of the body slumped next to me.

Ten minutes sat quiet I turned my head, saw Gloria with eyes closed, breaths slow and regular. I glanced at my watch. Time to leave, I had an early meet at the office. I eased away from the wonderful warmth of Gloria's body, untangled my fingers from hers, resisted the temptation to bend down and kiss her scarlet-painted nails, and left her peaceful and relaxed.

Plates and glasses stacked silent, washed and rinsed, Sleeping Beauty had not stirred. And Prince Charming decided to keep the farewell kiss stored for the right occasion lest it create a Dead Beauty in error. I left everything to drip-dry, gazed at Gloria to check she slept for real, thought of fetching a cover from her bedroom, realized that might freak her out to think I wandered around her boudoir. Instead I laid her coat over the near nude body, left the room on tiptoe, clicked the door shut, walked downstairs to my apartment after the best evening of my life.

In any normal boy-meets-girl scenario I would have met Gloria the next day on the stairs, or at a diner, or she would have knocked on my apartment door on her way to work in the evening, said a thank you with a smile and arranged a date for a drink. But this was Gloria Raccio. We didn't meet, accidental or deliberate. We returned to ships passed silent in day and night; me in the lightness, she in the darkness.

Just once our ships grazed hulls. I returned late from a drink with office colleagues, my eyes dragged along the sidewalk, thoughts lost on Gloria. And there she was, the opposite side of the street, arms linked with Detective Galvan, smiles spread wide, voices interrupted by chuckles and tightened grips, her walk staggered by, I guessed, gins bought by guys with no chance of buying anything more. Gloria and Galvan wandered on, oblivious to my existence. I watched them go, didn't want to imagine how the evening might finish, stuffed hands into my trouser pockets and gritted teeth for the journey home.

Seven

Several weeks passed by without a further sighting. Then footsteps started to land heavy overhead. Whether they were the tired ones of Gloria or the new heels of another Archie I couldn't tell. The latter seemed disappeared from the story, yet Gloria continued to inhabit the rooms upstairs, by default or as a permanent gift was a guess beyond my imagination.

But one place you might catch her Guerlain Shalimar was a bar.

'I ain't drunk, honey, give me another gin.'

The sentence my head lifted up from in the *New York Times*, a story about the Giants' inadequate defense, was forgotten fast. Nine at night, most guys just coming in to begin an evening's alcoholic show, and Gloria sounded twenty rounds ahead. I guessed she'd come through from a restroom or maybe an illegal poker table still with cards turned this early. The bartender hovered the spirit bottle high.

'One more. I don't want you upturned over the counter all night, it puts people off, Gloria.'

'I ain't drunk. I'm nicely loosened up. And I got bills and dimes for you.'

Gloria fumbled a silver clutch bag, coins rattled the teak. She counted out precise, slid the offering over toward the middle-aged bartender with a towel flung professional over his left shoulder. He counted every dime before he slurped gin into Gloria's dirtied glass.

She stood with elbows planted firm on the counter. A green dress, simple in its cut yet tight around the right places, stretched from neckline to kneeline. No coat or cardigan hung from an arm, just the clutch bag now lain slain on the counter, beaded strap spread over the edge, hung looped like a noose toward the shoe-scratched wood-planked floor.

I folded my paper, decided the coincidence of an encounter here gave an excuse to reignite our closeness of weeks ago. My chair had creaked back an inch when the backroom door opened. This time a small guy, about level-headed with Gloria, came through, left one arm wrapped around the door edge, lurched toward Gloria. My chair froze.

'Hey, girl, how long you gonna be? I paid for you till the game's finished. Johnny Bean's on a run, just flashed a royal flush down, hijacked five hundred dollars. Get back in here, I need a warm ass on my lap.'

'I need a break, Mario, a frigging break, I been pawed by you all night and day. Go grab Shirley's heinie.'

Mario, suited in something shiny and tailored mid-fifties, with black hair creamed flat and thick with a chin shadow at least a day old, stepped three times to draw alongside Gloria. By now the gin was about to embrace those cherub lips. Mario must have sunk a crate of warm Schlitz beer or a shared a gin bottle with Gloria, his feet clipped stools and floor on his short expedition along the counter. He collided like a bumper car with Gloria, nudged her enough for the gin to miss the eager-opened mouth. She swung around. Her palm slapped hard at the little guy's face. It caught a cheek and nose.

'My frigging gin, dumb head. I ain't coming, go put your paws on Shirley.'

The blow stopped the guy sharp. The hand, the look, the voice. All seemed to reveal another Gloria to him, not the pliant body he had no doubt enjoyed many hours out back or upstairs. His eyes flicked to the clutch bag. He took a pace back. Perhaps he feared she carried something lethal in the slim bag on the counter and sensed now she might use it.

The bartender, a bemused onlooker like the rest of the room, decided he didn't want a wreck of a bar to greet later clients. He sped around the bar, flung arms wide, pushed both sides apart, received no antagonized response, decided both parties were just too tired and over-alcoholed.

'You, guy from the Fifties' movie, upstairs, go lose another billfold, Gloria'll be up later. Go now or my Remington comes out from the shelf here.'

The guy, Mario, walked back two more steps, flicked gin from his hand, gave Gloria and the bartender looks worse than their bite, I hoped, and stomped off theatrically through the door. Gloria gave his back the finger, sucked wetness from her thumb, slunk back down on a stool and rested her head on an upraised palm supported by an elbow concreted onto the counter. I decided I'd try to enter her evening's storyline.

'Hey, Gloria, long time no talk. How you doing?'

She turned her head, eyes fought to focus against the drug of alcohol coursed thick through her veins, and frowned with concentration.

'I know you, buster?'

I sighed.

'Roy. From downstairs.'

'Shucks, so it is.'

She pulled herself upright, near toppled back off the stool. My hand shot out, gave support to a creased dress. Her back felt firm, warm, comfortable. I let my fingers drop away, with reluctance.

Gloria eased around to face me, ran a hand up through hair fallen loose from its salon-set style.

'Sorry, Roy, I been working so darn hard recent I don't even know my name these days.'

'Looked like you rub along with some tough guys, going by that one you slapped.'

'Huh, Mario? All mouth, no trouser, get my meaning? He's harmless, 'less he loses all night, then he gets trigger-happy with his Colt.'

My eyes must have widened with fright.

'Huh, no, he likes to shoot bottles and cans, not people. Mind you, a richo...richo...whatever, a bullet might go anywhere.'

40

'So, you still working the card games?'

'Shhh, meant to be a secret here.'

She glanced at the bartender. I followed her look. The guy grimaced serious, probably worried big guys in big suits might want to silence loose tongues, and the guy who couldn't keep the loose tongues tied silent.

'You cooked many meals since we ate together?'

Blankness flushed Gloria's face, then a memory seeped up through the gin-stewed depths.

'Ah, huh, no, not much. I sit in diners all hours. Shucks, we must do that again, it was fun.'

'Sure was. So, you and Olsen, that over, if you don't mind me asking, you were pretty upset last time we met.'

'Him? Best rid of the guy. All he wanted from me was information on Cigar Charlie, don't think he even saw my body in the bed.'

'What'd he want with Charlie?'

My legal mind caught up with my personal one. A PI interested in a renowned criminal?

Gloria flicked a finger at the bartender. He tossed a glass on the counter reluctant, poured a gin out halfway up. Gloria stared him down. He topped until the liquid rippled the edges.

'Charlie? Bobby wanted to take down as many of his goons as possible. Can you believe it? He got me a bruised cheek when he fed some cop friend details on a guy I worked with. Charlie coulda killed me.'

'Strange way for a boyfriend to act.'

'He were never my boyfriend, just a guy to take me to clubs and bars and shows. The shows sucked though, no songs in most. I like a good singer.'

'Me too. Maybe we could go catch a crooner somewhere sometime?'

Gloria swallowed half her drink in one go, didn't even notice the rough liquid razor over her throat.

'Why not? Sounds the bee's knees. Rattle my door some night.'

'You got favorite singers? I saw a few records stacked on a shelf in your apartment, never got time to look close.'

'Me? I like a guy or girl with a gravel voice, or someone who can take me to another place. Like Sinatra, Nat King Cole, Connie Francis.'

'Cool choices. There're good undiscovered voices in a few of the clubs around here. I'll find when one's on, we'll go, sing with them.'

'Huh, me sing? You wanna scare every tomcat in the neighborhood?'

I smiled, saw a smile spread on Gloria's face, it made mine spread further.

'You seem cheerful now, I was worried when you first came through to the bar.'

Gloria's face, bright and alive during the last minute, darkened like a child suddenly told she can't have the candy after all. She shifted on her stool. Her dress rose above the knee but she made no attempt to pull it down. Both hands wrapped around her small glass, twiddled it left and right.

'Like last time we talked, Roy. My life goes a long low, a short high, a long low. Your five minutes is the short high.'

I smiled again, at her words and the thought of being the 'high' in her life.

'Maybe we should make these five minutes longer or happen more frequent?'

Gloria released her glass, used one hand to prop up her chin while the other came across, touched my right arm light before it slid down to the counter.

'Ah, that's a good thought, Roy. But I ain't good to be with for too long, my head goes funny places.'

'Cut down the gin, might help straighten your mind.'

Gloria's eyes blazed playful.

'Gin's my oxygen! I can't go like Prohibition!'

My smile couldn't match the one wide and full on her face. It was a marvelous sight, even if it backed up a sad statement.

'Might be good to lead a normal life?'

Gloria held a hand out in mid-air between us, pointed a finger at me.

'Hold it there, I got a quote for you. What is it? Yeah, 'it may be normal, darling, but I'd rather be natural'. Cool, eh?'

My eyes widened. I stared at Gloria's proud-fixed face.

'You quoting me Capote? How the hell you do that?'

Gloria kept the finger stuck out, twiddled it at me.

'See, you ain't the only one can read words on paper. I got books on my shelves as well as records. You didn't see them 'cos you were too frosted eyeballing my body in my tap pants.'

The bartender looked up from drying wet glasses. A guy sat at the end of the bar glanced at me, reassessed the dull-dressed youngster he'd no doubt dismissed as a mama's boy.

Words stayed hung on my tongue. Surprised that Gloria remembered our time in such detail, surprised she thought I saw her like every other guy did. And still surprised she used words from Holly Golightly. Gloria's finger stabbed closer, touched my lips. Electricity capable of powering the whole Apple sizzled my body.

'And here's another one to roast you, Roy. 'You can love somebody without it being like that. You keep them a stranger, a stranger who's a friend'. Clever, eh? Like you and me, perhaps.'

Gloria's finger slid away, slow, careful, dribbled back across the teak-glossed counter. Like our love seeping away? Back inside our two selves after a moment let free out in the world? I chose the easier option of reply.

'What else you read in between hands of finger-greased cards?'

I kept my eyes locked on Gloria's. It took effort. I knew if I looked away I would color-up like a teenager on a first date with the quiet, long-haired girl from the classroom first row. If I'd tried to swallow, I would have choked on a thousand other words which might have shattered our fine-balanced relationship.

Gloria sipped gin. A responsible sip. Maybe to show she could control her addiction.

'I been dipped in Kerouac recent. You read *On the Road*?'

'You joking? You're reading that? You a beatnik in your spare time?'

My incredulity was genuine. To steal words from one writer, maybe thrown into the air by a well-read suit with his arms pulled tight around her waist during an interval at a play which bored her stupid, is one thing. To be sat with Kerouac on her lap was another.

'I don't recall you with a hand up in Miss Winspear's class, when we studied literature.'

'The classroom bored me frigid, Roy. I learn through life, then the words on paper mean something, if they're good words.'

'Gloria, you're wasted in these clubs, bars. You gotta get out, go to college, be something.'

Gloria threw out another of those glorious laughs, dismembered the world we all lived in.

'No, then I'd be like you all, you fool. I'd have no life to help me see the words' sense. 'The only people who interest me are the mad ones'. Kerouac got it.'

This girl quoted sharper than a Harvard professor. My love for a woman beautiful and on the wrong track of life blossomed into something more wondrous. To bander words of great writers, together with her own take on life, would be a life sculpted in Elysium. Yet in minutes she would be pawed and groped by fat-waisted suits who cheated on wives and kids like five-year-olds cheat at hopscotch.

I leaned forward onto the counter, clasped my hands together, stared at Gloria.

'What do you want from life? Really, strip away all that make-up, all the fast talk, all the clothes racked on wardrobes in different apartments?'

Gloria went for a rapid retort, shut off the words before they emanated beyond recall, found the surface of her gin a strange fascination.

'Nothing.'

I waited, thought she meant she had nothing sentenced in her head straight for reply. Silence lingered. I gave in.

'Nothing?'

'Nothing. Just live each day like it's the first, the last, my only twenty-four hours. There, that's an answer to get those psycho-whatevers to cross their legs and stroke their funny-pointed beards.'

'You don't want a home, a husband, kids?'

'Jeez, that's sad, Roy. That all you want?'

'All? Seems hell of a lot, I haven't managed one yet. Not quite.'

'But the routine. I'd be at home all day or swapping gossip in a store with housewives in scarves and with cream handbags and pushing a pram.'

'You'd rather...?'

'Not know what's gonna hit me tomorrow, fly on the moment, let the gin take me somewhere, let the music hit me high, let a handsome guy dance me silly.'

'And when the dance finishes?'

'I run off like Cinderella, but I keep both pumps on. Hah.'

The image made me smile, broke my interrogation. I stared at Gloria. She was flushed, in great spirits, different from the moment she had walked into the bar from out back. She was alive. With her thoughts, dreams, fantasies. I wondered where I could fit into them. Maybe when the gin wore off, when she sat on that sofa in the apartment, when she reached over and took my hand. That's what I wanted to manoeuvre toward, another time sat alongside her. And never to move from that moment.

Gloria leaned over again, nudged my arm with her fingers. Light, delicate, almost caring. Like a kitten wanting another game, another flick of the string, another roll of the ball.

'You gone quiet on me, Roy. That worries me.'

'Why?'

'Like I might have lost you.'

'You'll never lose me, Gloria. You want, I will be here for you always.'

'Now you're getting weird, buster. I told you, keep it like strangers, I can still love you.'

A thought, an idea, flashed my mind.

'What if I found you a job, say, in a coffee house, or a restaurant. Nothing near poker games, nothing near bars, nothing near guys in suits with guns holstered.'

'Honey, I'd be bored to stone, I'd be popping bennies like I did candy at seven.'

'Try it, you don't know. You hate what you do.'

'So do most everyone. You seen a happy worker? You seen a happy lawyer? You stare the sidewalks when guys walk home, I don't see many smiles. And I bet they sit on the sofas dreamed of the girl they missed, the opportunity they threw over for the safe job.'

Gloria finished her gin, ran fingers over her lips, sucked them dry of alcohol. Every guy in the bar must have stopped breathing at that act; it yelled more eroticism that an hour of striptease. She sank onto the stool, her stomach creased up, her shoulders slunk down.

'You know, I don't talk to anyone like I do with you. You're like the other half of my head.'

'Be kinda cool to talk every day?'

'My brain might fry! I'd drink a bottle of gin for breakfast, hah.'

The door behind the bar opened. A different man appeared; tall, thin, smart-suited with thick blond hair parted leftside, brushed neat.

'Gloria. Table two, now, Mr Eckstein's threatening to take his billfold down to Jimmy Spiro's.'

The guy's eyes spoke two or three more sentences you couldn't reply to. Gloria lost her smile, slipped off the stool, straightened her dress, fiddled with her bra strap underneath the material on her shoulder, slapped a hand on my arm.

'Catch me soon, Roy. I need saving.'

And she was gone. And I was a lonely guy at a bar with half a glass of whiskey.

Eight

The next I saw Gloria I was sat in Bamonte's over in Brooklyn. Dinner with my brother new in from Maine for a couple of days. My eye caught a figure stood by a table across the aisle. A red rose patterned cocktail dress fitted perfect around Gloria's body. She talked fast and furious with a guy and his girl. A shift of her hip and I made out Robert Olsen. I chuckled. My brother, Brian, looked up from a mouthful of steak, followed my stare. As did most of the room when Gloria's voice volumed higher. It seemed she thought little of Olsen's new woman, a dark-haired petite chick who could double for a young Audrey Hepburn if you excused her light brown skin. Gloria's hand extended, a finger poked at the woman's lips. Olsen's broad grabbed the arm, Gloria spat words with a sneer, the little lady swung an arm, Gloria caught it, twisted and parried like I had seen her do many times in the schoolyard. I gave a sharp intake of breath, prayed Gloria didn't swing her right fist, the Hepburn look would be ruined if her front teeth laid in the next table's turtle soup. Words replaced punches; I breathed out relieved. Gloria strutted to the main door, the eyes of everyone on her. I smiled, resisted the temptation to punch the air as if a home run had been completed.

Gloria disappeared from the apartment not long after. No sightings of her on the stairs, no reply when I screwed up courage to knock, no encounters in bars and clubs I really shouldn't frequent if I desired a reputation in a respected law firm. It was strange how one moment, one evening, we could be so close, physically and mentally, then go weeks with no contact. That was Gloria Raccio. Her terms, all or nothing.

Then, one Saturday morning, I strolled down to Carpenter's store to pick up a newspaper, the air whipped cool around my hatted head and ungloved hands. And there she was. One step out of a Buick, black and mean in looks. The car, not Gloria. She was in a dark blue coat, pinched tight at the waist by a gray belt. Black heeled

48

shoes, a couple of inches in lift, clipped the sidewalk. Her hair sat brushed and pinned, shiny in the early bright light of day, her make-up smudge-free. It looked no late-night escape into the next morning, more a fresh-out-of-bed-ready-for-the-day-ahead image in full battle formation.

My mouth began to form words, stuck open silent. A guy exited the driver's seat. The same tall, overcoated, fedora-hatted figure I'd seen in the poker room weeks ago. The one who pocketed a roll of dollar bills from Gloria. Galvan? Was that the name Dan had mentioned? A Floyd Galvan. A policeman. A detective. With dirty money bulged big in his jacket. Was Gloria arrested here? But then she wouldn't be stood by a car mid-town with the cop smiled broad. The two coupled arms, became a closer couple. I slipped behind people milled around a new display of televisions in a store window. Either they eyed the screens now twenty-one inch wide or the young woman bent down tight in a pencil skirt to arrange the terms of purchase. Gloria and her cop walked off the opposite direction. I forgot the newspaper, followed discrete. But I followed a detective. I guessed more than three streets, he would have me spread-eagled against a wall with large hands run up and down my jacket and trousers.

My lucky number proved to be two. They stopped two streets on. Galvan unlocked the door of an apartment block well-secured and glossed black. He stood back, allowed Gloria to walk through, followed with an arm tucked close to her back. The door closed. My surveillance ended. I could have leaned against a wall, imagined myself a Marlowe or Spade, or even an Olsen, but I wasn't getting paid. And Gloria might have moved from a collector of premiums to a lover in the intervening weeks.

Three days on I sat in a club I knew Gloria frequented; Dom's, the place to hear new voices sung in hope and new jokes cracked in desperation. The waitresses were middle-aged, did their job efficient, offered sisterly companionship to young and old, no flesh hung loose on view, no suited figures loomed with menace by doors. It had run for years, proof there was profit in law-abided normality.

I was on a second beer, my limit for a working night, when they came in. I recognized Gloria's laugh first. The deep gargle rumbled up from lungs flushed by a Lucky Strike or five. Galvan steered her to a table against a wall, slipped off the same overcoat I'd seen before, sat resplendent in an uncreased suit of gray. His fedora floated to the tabletop from fingers which signaled two drinks toward the waitress stood by the bar. Regulars it seemed, or at least he was.

The room was busy, moving bodies sheltered me from Gloria's view, and soon Dan's ample shape provided a shadow to glance from behind. Two hours I responded on automatic to my colleague's talk, my eyes fixed on Gloria and Galvan, my ears strained to pick up words spoken between them. When they exited, I made excuses, left Dan with thoughts he'd strained our friendship with a one-sided conversation, and headed out to track the odd couple.

Around a corner I near bumped Galvan into a lamppost. He was embraced with Gloria, arms circled tight, lips crushed with hunger. I glided away, found a doorway to spy from, like a younger brother who keyholed his sister necking with the bad boy down the end of the street. The kiss lingered, eyes stared deep, lips crushed again. It was the cliched end to a happy-sad-happy-again movie. I cursed. This was not bought time in a poker game or caressed evenings to earn dollars for food. This looked extra-curricular. This looked boy meets girl.

'Hey, long time no see you around, Roy.'

Books spilled from my grip, tipped end over end onto the carpet in front of my apartment. My gloves slipped over fingers, a scarf tried to flee from my raised-up neck. A figure shifted in my eyeline.

'Gee, you're like a new boy at school, got your mind on something?'

Gloria stood in front of me, at the bottom of the stairs where we seemed to rendezvous without preplanning. She had a smile spread so wide it lit the corridor from end to end. Her brown hair lay hand-brushed, natural and unlacquered, a soft cascade nestled on the collar of the red coat she favored. A dress, one shade darker, edged out from under the hem, and lead the eye down to a pair of sharp-pointed black kitten heels.

I abandoned the books, Gloria trumped them every time, and straightened up. My hat loitered one-sided, hopeful to cut me the dashing look of Cary Grant.

'You've not been over this way recently, Gloria, you startled me. You back permanent?'

'No, just wanted to see if I'd left a dress here, I got clothes stashed in wardrobes all over the Apple. What'd you call those folks wander the deserts all the time?'

'Nomads.'

'Yeah, that's it. Nomads. I'm like one of those folks. Saw a movie about them once.'

'So, you moved out the apartment upstairs? Archie told you to skedaddle?'

I kept away from Galvan. I didn't want my fears confirmed.

'Archie? He's out of town. Chased out, got himself on the wrong side of Krautz, the guy who runs rackets on the eastside.'

'You got free use of the rooms then?'

'Yeah, suppose I have, till some lawyer like your boss pastes papers on the door telling everyone to keep out.'

'And you good right now? Got work?'

Gloria had stood beamed happy all the time we talked. Her eyes sparkled. A cliched phrase used by poor-read writers, I know. But it described her look. Like a pregnant woman, their life's purpose on show.

'Me, Roy? I got better than that. I got me a guy. And not an Archie sort of guy. A straight guy.'

I fought desperate to keep my smile fixed and friendly.

'That's, that's just swell, Gloria. I'm pleased. I thought you looked different, sorta happy. He a man I know?'

Gloria leaned back against the banister.

'I hope not. He's a cop. Yeah, a cop. A detective. A good guy, bringing the bad ones down. Proper, not like Olsen with his snide whispers to college friends. A real deal cop.'

I fought down the lump risen large in my throat. Knowing the name to come didn't lessen the pain. And Gloria must know Galvan took bribes and payments, she handed bills over herself. I guess such small discrepancies still made her guy appear 'good'. Most she knew buried people in concrete or weighed them down with iron in the Hudson. Did I care so much for this woman that I tell her this man was just as bad as the ones he pursued? Or was my love for her so great I didn't seek to destroy her innocent dream of a happy-ever-after life? And who knows, it might work out. Galvan might quit the wrong side of the law; Gloria might become the housewife and mother she secretly dreamed.

'That really is good news. You, you and this guy, Galvan? You gonna share a place somewhere?'

'We hope. Floyd's got his eye on an apartment in Brooklyn, belonged to that man Krautz. He gotta sell, for tax reasons, you know. Floyd says he can get it for nada.'

'Sounds a useful guy to know. But his work's kinda dangerous. Maybe he can get a desk job, keep out the way of bullets.'

'Floyd? He tells others what to do, he don't go busting doors with his weapon waved angry, he's the boss.'

And nice and safe, his fingers deep in the pie made of deals signed with dirty handshakes and sly grins in penthouses inhabited by guys who paid no tax on their illegal gains.

'When you hope to, to move in? I can give a hand with your things if you like.'

'Ah, Roy, that's sweet. I might take you up on that. Floyd'll get a couple of uniforms to carry the boxes. Hah, imagine that, cops my servants.'

Gloria giggled, pulled her coat tighter, her cream handbag swung loose down her arm to her wrist. The stifled laugh made her cough, rattled and dry. My heart lurched to think of her deep entwined with a crooked cop.

'Hey, Roy, you got time right now, I need to shift a few of my records, Floyd has other tastes, you can take what you want. C'mon.'

I hesitated. Gloria turned, padded up several stairs. Did I want to be part of her parting?

'You coming, Roy, or your music gone all long and opera-like?'

'No, sure, sure, you caught me there, I hadn't seen you awhile then you say you're leaving.'

'I'm still in town, I ain't skedaddling to the West Coast like some half-wit actress.'

I walked up behind her, my eyes unable to avoid focusing on the sway of her hips even though clothed by her coat. My steps were heavy, nearly as heavy as my heart. Gloria, being a law unto herself, slowed, looped her arm through mine, drew me close. The Shalimar perfume smoothed over my face. Her lips landed soft on my cheek.

'That's for being you, Roy. The stranger I love. Who wanders in and out of my life.'

I blushed, swallowed, glad the corridor's half-light hid my face. Gloria pulled out keys from her coat pocket, took two attempts to unlock the door, walked in and flung her bag on the sofa. The sofa where we had sat, side by side, fingers intertwined. The spread-eagle strap of the clutch bag seemed to mock our moment of intimacy.

Gloria waved an arm toward shelves stacked untidy with leaned albums and books.

'Records are over there, help yourself, I've got the few I wanna keep.'

'You sure it's a good idea, you might want them back later, or...'

'Or what?'

'Things might not, you know, work out with...'

'Oh, don't worry about that, Roy. This is the real deal, we're gonna be circled and all. I'll invite you!'

I grinned in reply, no words would force themselves up out of my mouth. Gloria headed toward another door.

'Now, you find what you like, I'm gonna check the drawers in the bedroom.'

Gloria disappeared behind a green door, a tune hovered out of tune on her lips. I should be happy she was happy. But being a loved stranger was a killjoy role. My fingers flicked through record covers. I pulled out five or six, not so much for their contents, more to have something that Gloria's own fingers had touched, held, run over. A Miles Davis, a John Coltrane, a Bobby Darin, along with a Sinatra, Francis and Cole.

'You found anything?'

Gloria's head poked around the door, the delirious smile still fixed.

'Yeah, yeah, a few. Many thanks, I'll play them regular, think of you.'

'I said, I ain't going to the North Pole! I'll be around, see you in bars and places. Hey, might even call our first little one Roy! Hah.'

I guessed the horror I felt inside must have part-surfaced over my face.

'No, Roy, don't flip your wig! I ain't got myself pregnant. In the future, who knows, but not now. Shucks, your look, like you heard real bad news about the family.'

I stood up, the records clutched under my arm, not sure whether to wait, talk more, or leave, the thought of hearing more of this wonderful relationship a too depressing thought. Gloria made the decision for me. She came through with a small suitcase held in one hand.

'Hey, a favor, Roy. Can I leave the key with you? Someone'll come and collect it soon, an associate of Archie's. Can you be a chum and do that?'

Associates of Archie would no doubt be tall and wide with few words. But I couldn't say no to the girl. For anything. I took the key, felt the lingered warmth from her hand, wished I could varnish it permanent into the metal.

'You really sure about this? All of this? Galvan..., this apartment...? The records? You don't wanna take it slower, see how...'

Gloria took two steps, placed a finger on my lips, put another to her own.

'No more, Roy. Stop being my brother, or hell, my father. My choices, the right ones. Now, let's go, you lock up, you need to twist twice to the right to get it to click proper.'

We walked down the stairs side by side. What could I do? Drop the records, fall on one knee, ask Gloria to marry me? If it were the final scene of a musical or a romantic movie I might. Gloria would place her case and bag down, wrap her arms around my neck, kiss me and say she thought I would never ask, that I'd saved her from the biggest mistake of her life. Or she might look at me with pitiful eyes, realize how hang-dog smitten I'd always been, and walk out of my life forever.

'So grateful, Roy, see you in town, come over and talk, Floyd's a fun guy when away from work.'

Another kiss landed on my cheek. Then she was gone. The door shut behind her was a solid thud to period one chapter of my life. A chapter that could do with a savage rewrite.

Nine

Time passed as time does. No opportunity to stop, put it on hold, check what might or might not be a good choice. No chance to think back over mistakes, or moments when you could have said something and didn't try, never found out if it might turn out good.

And Gloria disappeared again. I heard Dan mention her name a few times, together with Galvan's, sightings he had had in bars and clubs. And once in a church. I think Dan might still have had ten beers in his head from the Saturday night before on that one. Or maybe Galvan was eyeing up the lead on the roof.

No one came for the keys to the apartment. After a week I gave in to temptation, went upstairs, unlocked, walked in. The perfume still lingered. A few records sat forlorn on the shelf. I gathered them up, my excuse if a large guy in a bulged suit shadowed the door. The sofa dipped in two places, I kidded myself it imprinted me and Gloria. The doorway to the bedroom was open. Inside it looked like it probably did on a Monday morning after Gloria had worked the club a full weekend, taken a lunch of liquids in here and thirty minutes slumber. A skirt hung in a wardrobe, a blouse laid in a drawer, a shoe hid under the bed, like a classic opening scene from a dog-eared crime mystery. I took nothing else, touched nothing else. Locks clicked, I left, more depressed than before I entered.

Galvan got mentioned in a couple of articles I read over the weeks. The heroic detective who broke up a protection racket then helped take down a gang who robbed banks for fun at lunchtimes, the busiest times of day. No mention of the monies he stowed in a well-stretched rear pocket or the blind eyes he must have turned to the illicit poker duals Gloria might still decorate.

At work I rocked back on a chair, my desk covered by a fan of paperwork I decided was too pretty to disturb. The office sat quiet early morning, most people out at calls or on way to court. A newspaper detonated like Enola Gay's bombload amid my typed forms.

'You haven't seen it, have you? You can't have, or you wouldn't be sat here so calm.'

Dan's action and voice had me wobbled on chairlegs already in need of a screwdriver.

'What the...?'

'Read it. The headline prepares you for the sensation.'

I steadied myself with a hand gripped on the table's edge, reached over the double-paged spread newspaper, took in bold-printed words.

'New York detective gunned down in Hagerstown.'

I turned to Dan who stood behind my chair.

'So...?'

'The name, first line underneath, the name.'

'Detective Floyd Galvan was gunned down in a park by shooter or shooters unknown on Wednesday. The police department would not comment...'

I stopped reading out loud. Floyd Galvan. Dead. In Hagerstown, Maryland. I swiveled in the chair, faced Dan who stood with folded arms and a stupid smile.

'You know any more? Why? Who? Gloria?'

'Nothing. Apart from the grapevine twanging that Bobby Olsen was in the park the same time.'

'Olsen? They think he...?'

'No, no, he tried to save Galvan. Had that sidekick beauty with him. Must have been a case the PI and the cops were both on. Hell of a coincidence otherwise, to have two arms of New York's good guys in the same town, same park, same time.'

'What about Gloria?'

'Not heard anything, nothing in the report there. Probably here in the Apple when it happened.'

'She'll be devastated.'

'Gloria? More likely she's got the next guy lined up for tonight. You better watch out, she'll be back at your apartment, fluttering those eyes, unbuttoning the blouse...'

My hands flew out, caught Dan full on the chest, a push, not a punch. He fell back, slid over the end of the next table, landed on his butt, bruised but unbroken.

'Jeez, I was joking. You know she's got a string of guys behind her. You still got a thing for her?'

I didn't answer; 'yes' would have brought derision, 'no' a blushed confession of a lie. The office double doors swung back with the force of my shoulder. The secretary at reception put a hand up to her horn-rimmed glasses, left her thick-glossed pink lips 'o'-shaped, and half stood to question my rapid departure.

Through heavy traffic it took me thirty minutes to get to the apartment I'd seen Galvan and Gloria go into together weeks ago. Repeated knocks got me nowhere. I stood across the street, hoped Gloria might see me from a window, let me in as a friend. Two hours I hovered. Then a black and white drifted into the street, pulled up by the curb outside the apartment's entrance. An officer got out, opened the rear door. Gloria stepped onto the sidewalk, shades on her eyes, coat collar pulled up tight. She fumbled at the door, overwatched by the cop, pushed her way in, then turned and thanked the officer. The car drove off down the street.

I rubbed a hand over my chin. It would be madness to go speak to Gloria now. I doubted she would open the door anyway. I hit a diner, filled up on eggs and a pressed ham sandwich, drank two coffees, drummed fingers on a grime-smeared plastic tablecloth. It was worth a shot. If Gloria ignored the knock I would try later in the evening.

No answer. I moved across to the opposite sidewalk, looked up at the window. A drape lifted with a hand, angled diagonal, dropped back straight. Seconds later the door opened an inch, a face peeked through the gap, a hand came out, ushered me toward the building. I walked over.

'Only for you, Roy. Quick, inside, before a newspaper guy spots another headline.'

Gloria's mascara, usually immaculate in application and effect, painted itself uneven and tear-streaked. Her lips bore color applied a day before and not renewed. Her dress, cream and cut for happier occasions with a cleavage low and waist-belted tight in brown, was rumpled and creased. She opened the door wide enough for me to slip past, our bodies grazed without a hint of feeling.

'Up the stairs, door's on the right.'

The hallway and stairs stood dark. Either Gloria was cautious in extreme to avoid alerting the outside world or she was too dazed to recognize the darkness. The main living room was spacious, furnished business-like and with more male touches than expected. This must be, must have been, Galvan's abode. Or maybe a safe place to hide away witnesses on the long hit list of a local gang. The sofa and chairs looked like they had been shifted out from a club, green leathered with dark brown wooden arms and legs. A drinks cabinet lined one wall, the others covered by artistic images of women dressed in fashions of the 1920s. Originals or cheap copies I had no clue.

Gloria dropped onto the sofa, collapsed back to lie along the hard cushions.

'There's only drink, the food's out, I ain't shopped a week or more, Floyd...Floyd and me ate out most times.'

I sat in an armchair which refused to give way to my weight and instead squeaked with indignation.

'Fine, cool, I just ate around the corner. Not sure you'd be here, happened to see you dropped off by the police, thought I'd give it a try.'

'I don't understand what Floyd was doing out there. He said he was put on a major murder case, couldn't move out the office for a week or more, said life was hell with threats of demotions if the perp wasn't nailed.'

'Could be he was on the case, following up a lead? Or perhaps he'd been told to give you and other folks that line, to put people off what he was really detailed to do.'

'You heard something?'

'No, no, guessing, what I hear in the office about other incidents. Could be nothing to do with those.'

'And I don't get what Bobby Olsen was doing there. And he tried to save Floyd.'

It was the first time I had heard Gloria use Olsen's familiar first name. I wondered if she still had feelings for the guy, she mentioned him so often. A gun to the head might not be the most caring way to call off a relationship but it was close to the way Gloria lived much of her life. Perhaps the memories had started to ring pleasant bells inside her maelstrom of a mind.

'The cops got a clue to who, who, you know, was behind it all?'

Gloria pinched her nose with two fingers, breathed in hard, folded arms across her chest, switched one leg over the other.

'They ain't told me nada. All they done is interview me, want to know where I was, what I was doing, who I was with.'

'And that's all cleared up straight?'

Gloria glared at me, the first strength I'd seen since coming in the apartment.

'Yeah, what you think? I gunned him down? What for? To get this place? He was the love of my life, the one, Roy. You get that? The one I was gonna spend the rest of my life with, have his kids, the house with the little white fence, you know?'

I let the volley wash through me, leave holes all over my heart. I sat shredded. Yet I still loved her. And wondered how long her pronounced devotion to Galvan might have survived.

'No, not at all, I didn't mean that. You know what cops can be like, they treat everyone as a suspect. It's their job, and it looks good in the newspapers, lots of people being interviewed, you know?'

The anger faded in Gloria's eyes, her head lolled back onto a light green cushion balanced precarious on the ridge of the sofa's back. Her eyes closed.

'Sorry, Roy, I'm cut up, that's all. I can't believe he's gone. I gotta go see the body, if they let me.'

Gloria turned her head toward me.

'You gotta go with me, I can't do it alone, you gotta be there, hold my hand. You will, won't you? Say you will?'

'Yeah, sure, I'll come with you, let me know when, where.'

The words came out even though my head swirled at the thought of seeing a dead body, especially that of a guy Gloria said meant the world to her. But I couldn't say no. She'd asked me, hadn't she? No one else. Or was that because I was the one here, at the right time, the right place?

'I knew you would. Remember, you're my stranger, the one I can love.'

'Sure, I'm here, always, Gloria. Hey, when you last ate? You need something, even if only a sandwich, got to keep yourself going strong.'

'I can't think of food. A drink, maybe. Pour me something large and frigging strong.'

I got up, walked to the cabinet.

'Make a deal, I'll get you a gin, you let me go get bread and cheese. Else I pour the alcohol down into the sewers.'

'Shucks, Roy, you play a hard game. I can go find a bar one minute from here, but I don't wanna be seen outside, so I give in. Give me the bottle, you go be mama in the store and kitchen.'

I put a half-filled glass into fingers shook with nerves. Outside I wondered whether she would let me back in, whether she might have sunk the rest of the gin bottle by the time I returned, whether she might even go and do something stupid. Fifteen minutes later, with a paper bag clutched tight under my arm, I approached the apartment apprehensive. But a swish of a drape and I knew Gloria waited for me. The door edged open then swung back, let me in, closed firm behind my back. She went up the stairs ahead, looked down over her shoulder.

'You cut up the bread and cheese, I'm gonna take a bath, wash out the cop stink. Put a record on, something sad and blue, have a drink, I'll be real quick.'

I stood in a tiny kitchenette, the space all gone on the living room, cut bread and pasted on butter slow. I was in no hurry to go sit down. Part of me worried Gloria might do something silly in the bath. Had Galvan left a razor in there? I listened to hear the splash of water, every sound relaxed my nerves an inch more. Another part of me worried she would walk out naked, throw herself at me, try to lose her sadness in a stupid five minutes which would forever ruin our friendship.

I was on my first drink, the sandwiches on a plate in front of me, when Gloria walked through. A dressing gown, scarlet and silk, wrapped itself like a second skin around her body. She walked to the sofa, sat down like a lady, legs crossed discrete, material pulled polite across her skin. I felt comfortable, confident the friendship would survive. Perhaps until a better time.

'That was quick, Gloria, you could've soaked away the day.'

'I was going to, then I got my thoughts in line, made a plan.'

'So fast? Best to review hasty decisions, that's my experience.'

'No, I know what I'm gonna do.'

I waited, hoped it didn't involve a move permanent out of the Apple. Gloria tucked her legs up onto the sofa, pulled the gown tidy.

'I'm gonna find the guy who wasted Floyd.'

It was the last option quick-fired through my head.

'You what?'

'The cops in Hagerstown won't put it top of their list. Yeah, Floyd was a cop, but not one of theirs. And Floyd always said precincts don't like to talk across boundaries. Especially since he...'

Gloria lifted a hand, nibbled a fingernail. The sentence hung unfinished. I gave in.

'Since he what?'

Gloria looked at me, then away, gazed at the drapes pulled across the windows.

'Floyd was like them all, willing to take a slice of moolah if it sped up cases quick.'

I could have added to the reasons but guessed it wise to our relationship not to. The same curtains became my focus, any connection with Gloria's eyes might reveal my knowledge.

'So I'm gonna follow up a few ideas, Roy. I might be away a while, if I find anything I wanna check out.'

'Let me know, maybe I can come help you. If it's all legal, of course.'

'Legal? Floyd was a cop, not much he dealt with was legal, Roy. You guys just pick up the pieces left over after the bust-ups.'

'Be careful, you don't wanna to find yourself facing the guy who shot Galv... Floyd.'

'I won't. I find out his name, I'll face his back, give him no chance to reply to my frigging statement.'

'And what would that be?'

Gloria raised her hand, pointed fingers at me, made a gun shape, shot an imaginary bullet my way.

'Bop. That's my statement. The sound of revenge.'

She was serious. Her face had no glimmer of playacting on it. A cold feeling ran down my spine.

'Not a good idea, really not, Gloria. I don't want to see you sat in the hot chair. Floyd wouldn't want it either.'

'I ain't planning to get caught. And anyway, I ain't found the frigging murderer yet, I might never, just run around then come back here. Least I'd have tried.'

'You find anything, you tell the cops. Or tell me, then we both can go to the precinct. I'll sit with you through it all.'

'I put you through enough, Roy. I find the man, I'll go tell someone, don't worry.'

I tried to think of reasons to add to stop Gloria's attempt at retribution but knew she would give a rapid answer to swat away my worries. Before I could work out what to do, she eased up off the sofa, pulled the gown's cord tighter around her waist.

'Now, Roy, I think you got work to do. A lady's gotta get changed and painted up.'

I stood up, put my glass down on a low table.

'Yeah, yeah, sure. Sorry, I should have vamoosed earlier.'

Gloria walked over, raised her hands, laid them on my cheeks, stared me close with her large brown eyes. Her freshness, the Shalimar washed away in the bath, was new to me, covered me from head to toe. Never had I felt the desire to kiss her more. Gloria beat me to it. On the cheek.

'No, I was glad you stayed, I needed someone to stop me shouting the walls down, you made me think, work out what to do. I can face it all now. But maybe you'll come to the morgue, see Floyd with me, when the cops say I can.'

I could hardly breath, Gloria was still stood so close. I would've done anything she asked.

'Sure, you telephone me, or put a note under my door, come into my office, anything, just let me know where and when.'

The words blurted out. Gloria smiled, her lips spread back over perfect teeth, her breath landed on my face, the most sensual thing I ever felt.

'Now, off, back to your books and papers, or I'll be asking you to hand me my clothes one by one.'

Gloria turned away.

'Shut the door firm on the way out, won't you?'

My reply probably never made its way up the stairs and through the wood before her door clicked closed.

It was no fun at the morgue. I was surprised the cops let Gloria in. Galvan had a wife and kids. His colleagues must have known about his affair, knew their colleague would have wanted Gloria there. I heard from an officer sat bored at a desk Galvan's wife shed no tears when she'd visited earlier, so maybe the marriage was over a long time ago.

Ten

Gloria disappeared again. As she so often did. But this time I worried sick about her. Never had I bought and read so many newspapers, feared to see a small column about a New York broad found gunned down in an alleyway or marched away between two handsome flatfeet (Gloria would insist on that) after shooting down a Mob hitman in a bar. The lack of news didn't quieten my head or my heart. Her demise might not even register worthy of newsprint.

Work began to dominate, a crumpled newspaper in a diner became my only possible link to Gloria. The apartment upstairs stayed quiet. A couple of times I went inside, checked the place over, reminisced about the time spent there. Each time the rooms seemed colder, dustier, lonelier.

Midnight on a Friday, the weekend loomed near, a date at a bar with Dan and two women from the office penned in the diary, knuckles rapped loud and urgent on my door. I walked more asleep than awake, eyes half-open, expected to find Cyril from next door in a panic over a tap dripped once more than normal. Instead I found a face stared at me like Helen on the day Paris said, 'Let's go away for a long holiday'.

'Hey, bad time to call you, Roy, but good time to see you.'
Gloria.

A coat, collar thick with fur, dyed deepest blue all over, hung well-fitted around her. Her face was bright, her smile happy and genuine, her cheeks rosy.

'Gee, Gloria, what a sight you are. Thought I was still in a dream.'

'Why you look so surprised? You got a girl in there with you? You talked her into bed with your words of clauses and appendices? She got a flat chest and legs like tree trunks?'

Her rapid-fire sentences dazed my head. I pulled the door wide open, let her into the hallway, closed up behind her lest the whole block think I called out women for late night entertainment.

Gloria swept through into the living room, peeled off her coat, dropped it over the back of my heavy-creased leather sofa. I trailed in, retied the cord around my dressing gown, shabby and aged compared to her outfit.

'Well, Roy, sorry about the late time but I kinda need to keep out of the limelight right now.'

She stood by the sofa, pulled off white gloves, brushed down a hand over the black two-piece suit she wore. The buttons blazed bright, large statements on a plain business-like design. Her hair had loosened from a pinned-up style so often seen in theaters and expensive restaurants, strands cascaded down her cheeks and over her ears. Her make-up looked hours old but retained the sharp edges seen on the front of glossy magazines.

'It's fine, Gloria. I'm happy to see you anytime, anytime at all. You want a coffee?'

'Yeah, if you haven't got that woman waiting in the bedroom.'

Her smile played playful. I wondered if she had popped a bennie or something stronger, she seemed floated on some far distant high plain. But night-time was her time, maybe she'd come straight from a high-rolled poker table, still burst with the adrenalin to induce shy suits to part with bills.

'No woman in there. Just a dream or two.'

In the kitchen, I fired up the coffee maker. Stood in pajamas and dressing gown, I felt foolish, like a father waited up late for his stay-out daughter.

'Give me a moment, Gloria, gonna throw clothes on.'

'Don't bother, I kinda like you looking homey.'

I walked into the living room, headed to the bedroom.

'Thanks, I prefer a classy look like a Grant or Hudson.'

'Shucks, Roy, don't aim too high, you'll put yourself outta my class.'

I tore pajamas off, slipped on a shirt and pants, put feet in slippers, padded back to the burbling coffee machine.

'You want something to eat?'

'No, I'm filled up on diner food, been driving around quite a while.'

'Didn't know you drove?'

'Huh, honey, I don't, and the guys I weaved around probably guessed it too.'

'Why you out in a car then?'

'Helped me think, nothing more.'

Gloria's voice had dropped quiet. I frowned, wondered what she might be hiding. Robbed a bank? Run off with the poker takings? Were a mob of Cigar Charlie's goons going to kick down my door? I decided to go a roundabout route to the truth. Not that I might wish I hadn't.

'You been working tonight?'

'Nope, out and around, that's all.'

'With a guy?'

'You jealous if I said yeah?'

I hesitated in reply. Quick-fired dialog can cut too close to the truth.

'Only if they're more a dreamboat than Cary Grant.'

'You got a thing about that guy? You keep mentioning him. No, no guy, me and me alone.'

I took the coffee into the living room. Gloria sat spread-happy along the sofa, relaxed as if she were in her own apartment on a Saturday afternoon. It was a while since I'd seen her so contented, she seemed to have come to terms with Galvan's loss. Or maybe it was whatever she might have consumed earlier in the evening. She took the cup I offered, fixed a look on me and gave one of her 'I-can-break-your-heart-smiles'. I sat down in an armchair opposite her.

'You headed up to the apartment? I checked it a couple of times, all's quiet and tidy.'

'Tidy? You must've given it a clean over then, I ain't never been accused of being tidy.'

'You passing through? Why stop here so late? Not that I'm not happy to see you, always.'

Gloria drank long from the coffee, hot though it was, held the cup in both hands as if to warm herself.

'I feel good tonight, I had to share it with someone I care about, didn't wanna be alone, drunk stupid in a bar with guys throwing dollars and hands at me.'

Sank into the chair, I blinked to keep myself awake, the initial adrenalin of Gloria's unexpected appearance siphoned away to leave me desperate for sleep yet desperate with curiosity as to why she was here.

'So, coffee with a dull friend came up on the dice throw?'

'Dull? You're never dull, Roy. A little predicable, yeah, but you with a regular daytime job, well-ordered life, career ahead, you're anything but dull to me. You're a crazy guy, such a life!'

Gloria rocked back on the sofa, kept the cup level with effort, put a hand up to her mouth to stop coffee revisiting the room.

'We drinking the night away here, or you need a roof, or you disappearing off somewhere?'

'You kicking me out? You have got another broad here, haven't you?'

Gloria swept to her feet, walked brisk to the bedroom door with the cup held firm in one hand. She pushed the door open, stepped inside. I could have followed, once my head got over her quick move, but I wondered what might happen if we stood close in a room with a bed. The armchair anchored me safe.

Gloria turned, leaned against the doorframe, clasped the cup again with two hands.

'I'm disappointed, thought I'd discovered something naughty about you. Or you saving yourself for someone?'

'Yeah, someone. I got to get sleep, Gloria, sorry, I'm happy you're here, really, but I...'

Gloria walked over, went down on knees in front of me, the cup left behind on the low table in front of the sofa.

'Shucks, I don't mean to crash your life, Roy. Can I stay here, on the sofa, just tonight, I don't wanna go upstairs, be alone? I'll be good, won't drink, or sing, or wander in to cuddle up tight. Please, let me stay, till morning, then I go, promise.'

Her change of voice, back to the one lacked in confidence, the little girl lost, threw me. I didn't know what to say. But knew I didn't want to send her away, even if it meant a night with her so close by.

'Sure, sure, stay. I'd like it, it won't be a problem, honest.'

Gloria's face beamed again, like a kid who's been told Santa Claus has left her an extra present, in the paddock.

'You mean it? You're a brick, Roy!'

She moved forward, lips smacked mine. The warm, lush flesh of hers were there but a second yet imprinted me for a lifetime. Words coughed up out of my mouth in single letters, forced themselves to join together as they met the fervid air between our so close faces.

'I'll get blankets, a cover, a pillow.'

I stood up, Gloria did likewise. Our bodies were an inch apart. Her warmth swept over me, sent me giddy. I pushed my legs back against the chair to keep myself upright. Her hands reached out, grasped my wrists. Her eyes held mine, unblinked and sincere.

'Remember, Roy, forever strangers in love.'

Eleven

Sleep avoided me that night. Gloria's sudden appearance, her flushed state, her wish to stay, her actions and words. They all swirled inside my head like a merry-go-round, bells and lights flashed loud and bright. The fact she slept just one wall away played on my mind too.

Sometime in the early morning I drifted away into dreams. When I awoke, I found the sofa empty, the cushions arranged neat, the kitchen wiped clear. I couldn't see a note scrawled in lipstick on tabletop, window or newspaper. Isn't that how it would be in the movies? A dramatic close-up of declared love, the writer never to be seen alive again? Maybe Gloria found the words too hard to put into print, afraid they might convey a strength of feeling too strong. Or too weak.

Routine closed up the moments of wondering where she was, what she was doing. Work suffocated me, stopped me wandering the bars and clubs I knew she'd frequented or worked in, left only the last minutes of every evening to turn over that last visit of hers.

Three long days snailed past.

I bought a newspaper on the way to work, a frontpage story about Gary Powers' continued imprisonment in the Soviet Union eyed up for reading later. Sat hunched at my desk, pen in hand, the noise of the office drifted away.

'Hey, Roy, you seen this?'

Dan dropped a newspaper over my shoulder, let it fall on top of the letter I was composing to a client. My hand deflected it off the wet ink. The one-hundred-year-old firm I worked for still required handwritten documents to introduce our services to potential new customers.

'Seen what? Careful, I've written this letter twice already. And next time ask before you steal my newspaper.'

'What's the point of buying it if you don't read it early? News gets old by midday.'

'I'm sure Powers will still be locked up somewhere unpleasant.'

'Inside, you dolt, page two, remember that guy who worked for Olsen?'

'Olsen? Bobby Olsen?'

A hand clipped my combed hair, disturbed the light-creamed top layer.

'Blockhead, no, his father, Old Slab Sides, the one gunned down in his home. I'm talking about the guy it was rumored was one of his illegitimate sons.'

'Oh, him. Yeah, vaguely.'

'Bruce. Nasty type, said to be trying to keep the old Olsen gang going, cops were interested in him over various protection rackets.'

'I remember, yeah, Bruce. Didn't he come in here once, wanted representation or something?'

'I don't know the details, but he did try to get an appointment. And the suits upstairs showed him the door, threats or no threats.'

'What about him? He running for mayor? Or president?'

Dan reached over, flipped the newspaper pages across my desk.

'There, the guy's been found dead, riddled in a back alley. Could be a mob hit, that's one of the newspaper's angles.'

'Okay, and why's that important to us?'

'Read it further on. Bruce was suspected of being involved in the murder of the detective, Floyd Galvan, over in Hagerstown. The reporter also throws out the idea maybe another cop took justice into his own hands, murdered the guy, shot him down in the back.'

'Thought you said it was a mob hit?'

'Nah, just the paper filling out paragraphs. The mob would've put him at the bottom of a river. I reckon we got a rogue cop, with a group of brothers-in-arms behind him. Good riddance, I say.'

I sat quiet. My head ran patterns a football coach would never try out.

'When was he killed?'

'Galvan? A few...'

'No, no. This Bruce guy.'

'About three days ago, body was found early, probably shot late night, before or around midnight.'

'Holy moly.'

A pattern just saw my wide receiver gallop over the end zone. I pulled the newspaper closer, read every word, reread the paragraph detailing the timing of the murder.

Gloria.

The times fitted. The motive fitted. Hell, the motive screamed out in letters larger than the Hollywood sign. Surely the police knew it too. Some must have known of Galvan's affair with Gloria. Eyes were averted when we went to the morgue. And it would be perfect for them. A known cop murderer killed and none of them directly involved. Gloria's only worry was if someone saw her or a cop went honest. And she'd come straight to my apartment? Was the murder weapon on her while she slept feet away from me? Bruce's blood splattered on that dark suit?

'Thanks, Dan. I gotta go out, got a letter to deliver. Catch you at the diner.'

'Out now? We got a meeting with...'

I was gone. Out the office door, out the entrance past the receptionist, out onto the sidewalk among the melee of striding suits. I walked nowhere. Just walked and walked and walked.

An Italian coffee house ended my sojourn, quiet and without music. A pretty waitress placed a coffee with care in front of me, smiled sweet and padded off without a sound. The very opposite to Gloria and her hustle and bustle and mayhem of a life. I ought to return to this place soon, make dialog with the waitress, take her to a romantic movie. She was just the girl to make my Ma smile glorious with dreams of the kids we would produce. But Gloria's laugh spread wide inside my head, mocked my image of the picture book perfect partner.

But how to find Gloria now? She must have quit the city, gone west, north, south. As far as possible away from any uncovered-up clues or stared eyes. Maybe out the country even. I didn't know where to start. Wait and see? Forget her? Come back here, flash eyes at the quiet, pretty waitress?

I reached the office ten minutes after the meeting finished, explained my absence on a bad pizza the night before, got a lecture from a sixty-year-old partner about the advantages of home cooking, preferably by a house-proud wife. The rest of the day went by without incident. I shut out Gloria with the minutiae of business law and the endless drafting of a letter not allowed to be posted until my superior had checked every word like an over-zealous college lecturer.

At home, in the quiet emptiness, she rushed back into my vision.

Gloria had said nothing that evening to make me think she'd committed any crime. If the cops came to visit, I would only have the innocent truth to tell. Dan would support me over his declaration of the news. The fact I'd put two and two together, made a possible headline-shattering four, had to remain inside my head. But there was no reason why I couldn't drift around a bar here, a club there, just see if she turned up, or a hostess mentioned her name. The chances were I would get a rap of small feminine knuckles on my apartment door at a crazy time before I ever caught sight of Gloria's brunette locks.

Twelve

'You still frequenting this place, Roy? Thought it'd be out your billfold reach?'

Dan. I couldn't escape him at work or at play.

'Just curious, about the game, never really understood poker.'

'And here's a safe place to learn? A club where it's probably not all legal, where one peek over a shoulder might get you more than a sharp elbow in the stomach, where the guy on the door's biding time before riding shotgun on a bank raid at midnight?'

'It's cool here, not that bad. I like the atmosphere. Kinda like a noir movie.'

'You got that right. I keep expecting Bogart and Hepburn to be hung at the bar.'

'How often you been visiting here, Dan, in recent days?'

'Too often, been talking a black-haired waitress into stepping out with me to the theater next week.'

'Theater? You?'

'Turns out Mary, the lady concerned, is a budding actress, just earning dollars here while treading the boards down at the Martin Beck Theatre.'

'So you recognize the girls working here?'

'Ah, the real reason you're here. Which one you got your eyes on?'

Dan's slapped hand on my arm pushed me back a step. I smiled, didn't want to deny it, thought it'd be better to let him think I had intentions on one of the waitresses meandered slow around the three tables and the chairs and stools ranked along the walls. The clientele appeared less well-cut in suits tonight. I guess the management dribbled in profits on a few nights from a rapid turnover of billfolds less swollen.

'Not a particular one. The redhead's kinda cute, and a brunette, but she doesn't seem to be here.'

'Brunette? I've seen several here over the weeks.'

'The one who seems to run the bar when she's here, talks to suits who come through the rear door.'

'Yeah, think I know that one. Hell, Roy, you're a quiet one. You mean Raccio, don't you? Gloria Raccio. The one you talked about that other time. She looks real danger, a chick for sure but I bet her fingernails are razor-sharp. Maybe aim for the redhead, she's over on the far table with the old guy in the gray suit.'

I pretended interest in the tall broad whose figure cut a mirror image of Jayne Mansfield. The man with the cards and the chips didn't seem to know where to look, at his clutched pictures or the swelling bosom rubbed up close to his arm. I kept my eyes on her, a smile of false appreciation on my face.

'And the brunette. You seen her the last couple of days?'

'Well, wasn't here yesterday, me that is. Can't say I have, but then she isn't the one I come for.'

'You heard any more on that killing of the detective? Doesn't Mr Schneider, your boss, do a lot of criminal cases over the precinct?'

'Don't think he's involved in that one. Guys talk about it over the desks, Schneider joins in, especially when Winkleman comes over from the firm next door. Talk centers around a rogue cop, now protected by a wall of badges and caps. Keep a lookout in the bars they frequent for a guy who doesn't have to buy his drinks. My bet is he's the hero.'

'If that's true, I guess the case will be closed quietly, forgotten all about?'

'Probably has already. Next big scandal or murder will push it back into the dusty shadows.'

The redhead sashayed to the bar, her elderly Don Juan had pulled on an overcoat and headed to the door. Maybe a nurse waited somewhere with his medical nightcap. I saw an opportunity.

'Just gonna break the ice.'

I walked to the bar, stood next to the waitress leaned over the counter, chin cupped in hand, eyes stared blank at the rows of bottles hung upside down.

'Hey, can I buy you a drink?'

A lame opening but time was short.

The redhead swiveled her head like a tiger who caught sight of prey. Very small prey, but maybe worth a one-bite gulp as an appetizer before the next main course entered the room.

'Ain't allowed, honey. You got to be at a table, spreading high bills over the cards, before you can do that.'

'Sure, thought so. I wondered, as you seem to got a free moment, if I could ask about one of the other waitresses?'

Long fingers slid a Winston into her purple-painted lips, a Zippo fired to life, a steady inhale flared the cigarette's end red and black. Smoke raced out nostrils with the slightest upturn. Her eyes held mine, peeled me bare, decided I was out of my depth and therefore harmless.

'Which one? And I ain't giving out addresses.'

'Yeah, sure, anyway, I know where she stays some of the time, in my own block. But I haven't seen her around, getting kinda worried.'

'Describe her, honey. I think I know which one you're hunting, but you prove me right first.'

I ran out words to paint Gloria perfect, tried to keep them plain and honest with the ones expressing my hopeless love hidden away out of sight. The redhead nodded, dragged deep again, let the smoke drift up around our heads. If I'd been here to talk her into dinner, it would've been an erotic moment, smoke from inside this bombshell mingled around my mouth and nose. Odysseus must have felt the same when Circe tried to seduce him into a life on all fours in a pig pen.

The redhead looked me head to toe again.

'She's gone, least for now, you best go find another broad to go soppy over.'

'We talking about Gloria?'

The woman nodded, picked a piece of cigarette paper or tobacco off her lips with a finger long-nailed and glossed a color to match her lipstick.

'We are. Got some stuff going on. Maybe she'll be back, next year, next decade. If you know her, you know she comes and goes on her own terms.'

'Yeah, I realize that, I've known her a while.'

'Forget her, honey. You got more dollars in your pocket than you look like you might, you can spend time with me. Here or back at my apartment.'

Her legs swung around on the stool, poked out from the split in her red dress, crossed one over the other, showed off calves slender and shaped perfect, finished off in a pair of stilettoed dark red shoes. She seemed to sense easy earnings from a guy on the rebound from unrequited love.

I smiled, looked down at the counter, caught the glance of the waitress behind the bar who poised to fill the order I should've put in by now if I wished to remain in the room.

'Not for me. But I appreciate the offer. Thanks for your time, I'll leave you to find a guy with a greater stash of bills in their jacket.'

I eased away from the bar. The redhead didn't reply or move her head. I guess I was forgotten before I made the second step back toward Dan.

Thirteen

A month drifted along. The odd excursion to the poker game, a walk into the bars I knew she haunted, a meal in a diner I once saw her in. Nothing. And nothing in the newspapers to suggest the case of Bruce's murder was still ongoing. After the report of his death there hadn't been a word more printed. If it had been Gloria, it looked like she was in the clear. From the cops. But I wondered if any of Bruce's associates, or family if the rumored connections were correct, might not still be on the trail of his killer.

One Monday night, work gone easy for a change, I sat in a restaurant on Staten Island. Not a place I frequented but I'd taken paperwork over to an office colleague who had cried off sick for a long weekend. Now he sought to make up time before he returned with excuses run practiced over an alcohol-bristled tongue. The restaurant room hummed with quiet dialog; couples leaned close over the white-clothed tabletops exchanging future visions, singles stared out at the sidewalk after each tasteless mouthful wondering why they had no one, a group of six celebrating something significant with smiles and backslaps.

My dessert of bananas Foster sat smug in temptation on a dish. Then something wafted through the air that hadn't originated from the menu card. I kept still. The perfume was popular. A thousand girls must be adorned in it right now. I wanted to turn. But didn't want my highed hopes thrown out, either by the appearance of a dark-haired slim broad or Gloria hung off the arm of yet another rich suit or downtown overweight goon.

The dessert began to melt before my eyes. I watched sweet rivers slid down the banana. Then a body slid down into the chair opposite me. The air expelled from my lips near caused an avalanche of sweetness to burst over the glass dish.

'Well, well, Roy, you gone all high class on me now? You got a daughter of a congressman lined up as your partner?'

My eyes met Gloria's. And took in the new version. Hair now shaded black, the waves straightened looser, the make-up less pronounced, the clothes monotoned but smart.

'That you, Gloria?'

A stupid opening line. It wasn't a query over the person in front of me, more a question to myself. Could she really have reappeared like I dreamed so many times?

'Huh, yeah. Change of color here and there, a girl's gotta keep the guys guessing, hasn't she? How's your life?'

Gloria shuffled the chair forward under the table, placed her elbows on the cloth, pyramided fingers now tipped in pale pink. Lips parted in a smile, the perfect teeth flashed beneath. The old Gloria broke to the surface. I stared at the face, familiar despite the changes. My fingers clutched a spoon upright.

'It's you, isn't it?'

I sat back, my mouth open in relief and disbelief. The spoon dropped to the table cloth; a chuckle dropped from my lips. Gloria smiled a smile I recalled over many years.

'Yeah, it's me, fat-head. You wanna me go dance on the tables, give everyone a version of Brenda Lee's 'Sweet Nothin's'?'

She leaned across. The sides of her dark blue suit jacket spread wider, revealed a similar blue blouse underneath. Very Manhattan. The cynic in my head whispered she dated a guy sat high up a skyscraper office.

'No, no, sorry. I just...I just been hoping you'd be back..., sometime..., maybe later in the year...'

'Why, Roy, you miss me?'

Gloria unpeeled a hand, extended a finger toward me, placed it on the end of my nose. Her eyes locked mine. I felt a shiver go through me top to toe, felt like a dog home after lost for days, the hands of its master wrapped loving around its neck.

Gloria's finger stayed there. And stayed. Her eyes remained on mine. This was more than a playful gesture. Was it a question? A test? Of loyalty? Of more?

I spoke with the touch still in place.

'Of course I did. I do. I hate it when you disappear, don't say when you might return, don't give an address or something.'

Gloria's finger slid down to my mouth, stemmed the flow of words. Again it stayed still, rested on my lower lip.

'Shhh, you don't want the whole restaurant know you're devoted to me, do you? That'll be like a declaration of something, wouldn't it?'

To reply would've meant disturbing the finger. I wanted it to stay there for ever. The temptation to let it slide inside my mouth was there, thumped inside my head. Instead I reached up, held Gloria's hand, moved the finger barely half an inch away from my lip.

'Did you, did you have anything to do with the killing of Bruce, the guy they say shot down your Floyd?'

Gloria didn't flinch, didn't move a muscle. I felt nothing through the finger I grasped, no contraction, no extra pulse of blood. Her eyes stayed steady, no dilation or flare of the pupils. Maybe the lack of any recognition of guilt or apparent recollection of the event said it all.

'Why would you think that, Roy? I can't get beyond my loss of Floyd. But he's gone. I have to move on, I can't live the future with my eyes locked on the past. And I'm sure that guy Bruce had many enemies, not just among the police. Someone would get him, somewhere, sometime.'

I held her look. If I moved my eyes away, I was afraid I'd show doubt, a dent in my belief in her.

'I had to ask, you turned up not hours after they say he was gunned down, it crossed my mind...'

Gloria's other hand came up, grasped mine, her fingers tight around my skin.

'Don't worry about it, the cops thought the same, not official, of course, but one came around, asked me a few questions, and, well, look at me now, I'm free and easy, ain't I?'

'They did? Swell, you know, if everything's cleared up. They say who they suspected?'

'Nada. But they never do. Between me and you, Roy, I think it was one of them, getting revenge for Floyd, you know what they're like, the cops, closer than those stuck together twins.'

'Yeah, could be. Guess no one will ever be sat in the chair for the crime then.'

'Whoever they are, in my book they're a frigging hero. And if you'd bought me a drink, I'd raise the glass to them right now.'

I moved back, let my hand slide away from Gloria's, sat upright.

'Sorry, you want something? Grab a meal here with me?'

'You know, that would be real good, and maybe we can talk about the future.'

Gloria picked up a menu card, ran a nail down the list of options. I took a sip of water.

'Future? You sticking around here? Disappearing again somewhere? What do you mean?'

Gloria raised a hand toward the waitress, waved her over.

'I'll take the pineapple and celery salad, and make it snappy.'

Gloria dismissed the young woman with a gesture of her hand, as if she were used to dining at Sardi's or PJ Clarke's.

'Roy, I got a plan. For us. But now, we eat.'

I took a mouthful of my melted dessert, swallowed slow, watched as Gloria took off her coat, walked over to the row of pegs on the wall, hung it up. She came back with a stroll that caught the eye of every man in the room, a swagger of one who owned the whole caboodle. A graceful slide back onto the chair, the dark skirt tucked neat under her legs, her fingers started to tap an upbeat tune on the tablecloth.

The food arrived, placed curt but polite by an unsmiling waitress who hadn't been fooled by the tone of the order, the Apple-sliced accent having voiced away the customer's background all too clear. We ate on, small talk about food, the décor, the weather, a pair of men who entered loud and brash, a lone middle-aged woman, a regular couple out for a meal away from the kids.

Cutlery placed together on the plate, Gloria dabbed her lips with a napkin, dropped it by the side of her glass, let our conversation stall. 'A plan for us' reverberated round my head; it had for the course of our idle talk. Gloria seemed famous for having no plan, and as for an 'us', it appeared to consist of a closeness for an hour or two then weeks of distance, often measured in miles.

'Roy, let's get out of New York.'

I looked at Gloria. She gazed straight back, hands clasped together in front of her on the table. My glass of water twiddled between thumb and forefinger.

'Tonight? Where do you want to go? Why? I gotta be at work first thing tomorrow.'

'I ain't talking about one night. For ever, all time, never come back.'

My grip tightened around the glass.

'Just like that? Out of the blue? Leave?'

'Yeah, why not? You and me, go set up some place west, as far west as we like.'

'First, you wouldn't last two days outta the Apple, second I'm not qualified yet, I can't walk into a job elsewhere.'

'But I've got moolah, Roy, that gives us, you, time. There's no rush, you can find another firm, finish whatever you have to finish, set up like a regular Perry Mason.'

'Money, Gloria? From where? Or shouldn't I ask?'

Gloria leaned across the table, lowered her voice.

'Floyd. He left me the apartment and more. The account he'd set up to finance our affair and eventual life together. I heard last week, all official, from a lawyer like you guys, it all becomes mine end of the month.'

I picked up the glass, drank long. And drank in the details Gloria had fired at me out of nowhere. Another scheme she'd plucked out of thin air with her painted fingertips? Destined to last two, three days then be abandoned on the sidewalk? Along with me?

'You listening, Roy? I ain't kidding around, things have changed for me. I told you Floyd was serious about him and me, he's set things up even though he's gone. Now we got a chance to start right, the two of us.'

'The money's kosher? You aren't gonna get a detective come around at midnight to demand it back? Or Floyd's wife turn up with a couple of lawyers? Or a Cadillac full of Cigar Charlie's goons drift up slow beside you on a street, bundle you away to a dark alley or shoot you down on the sidewalk?'

Gloria slumped back in her chair, a smile so wide it threatened to split her cheeks. Her voice kept low.

'Nothing. Nada. Zilch. It's what we were gonna use for a new life, separate from his wife, his soon to be ex-wife. She don't need it, she'd been left plenty, a pension, whatever, the house, you know. You, Roy, you and me, we get along like an old circled couple, we were meant to be together, you've had a crush on me since the schoolyard.'

The flush that dropped like shades over my cheeks could be read throughout the room. A face or two had turned our way despite Gloria's quiet tones, her extravagant emotions hinted at either a lovers' argument about to burst banks or one of us to stand up and pronounce unending love for the other.

Gloria bounced off the back of the chair, reached across, grasped my forearms with tight fingers, the nails close to knife-points on my bare skin as they slid under my shirt sleeves.

'You gotta believe me, Roy. There's only one person I wanna share everything with. Yeah, with Floyd I would've gone his way, but only because he seemed to protect me against people here. Now I can leave. With you. We make a great team. Better than the Nicks any season!'

I tried to breath slow, stop the heart hammered hard against my ribs, against the table edge, darn it. A dream come true was about to come true for real, not just in a neat phrase. To spend my life with Gloria was everything I wanted. Now it was here, it seemed. It just wasn't how I expected it to come about, it wasn't me with the initiative, whisking her off to the sunset horizon with the movie credits rolled. A horizon only a few blocks away, I admit. My dream took her to an apartment here in the city, to a life revolved around places we knew; theaters, bars, restaurants, parks in the Apple.

Gloria's fingers remained on my arms, holding tight, a warm connection. My eyes stared at hers. Neither pair flickered.

'We need to talk about this, not here, after a night's sleep, tomorrow, to give me time.'

'I get that, Roy. But, if you had to choose right now, no time, no pillow to rest your head on, what would you say? Give it me straight.'

And I did.

'I'd say yes.'

Gloria leaned back again, dragged her hands down my arms, entwined her fingers with mine.

'I knew it! Knew you loved me! Always did. But I'll give you time, just don't go writing down two lists like a legal document you do at work.'

'I've loved you since I first saw you, Gloria. I can't deny that. And I've dreamed of you and me being together for years. But, I can't quite believe you want this. It's almost too much, so unexpected, out the darn blue and all that.'

'That's me, isn't it? Everything out the blue. Keeps life fun, huh? Never a boring moment if you've got your arm linked through mine.'

I sat there, hands held across a table, like a regular couple. Crazy. I squeezed Gloria's hands with gentle pressure.

'So, what now? Meet up tomorrow, decide what we do?'

Gloria shrugged.

'Yeah, sure, my time's my own now, I ain't working in no club, not less I own the place. Or, we could go back to your place, you know...?'

The look in her eyes melted me. Fingers and toes tingled. But my head kept straight amid the chaos.

'Let's, let's take it slow. I came here for a quiet meal, it looks like I leave with the most beautiful girl in the world on my arm. I feel like I'll wake up, find it's all in my imagination.'

Gloria chuckled, dipped her eyes, gave me a half-lidded look that near flipped my decision to delay a few hours.

'That's cool, Roy. And you're right! As usual. You're gonna keep me straight, I'm gonna keep you laughing. What a couple we be!'

'How about, we meet at mine, tomorrow, around seven?'

'That's a date! Don't you be stuck late in that gray office of yours, or I'll come over, drag you out, and I'll wear my sexiest outfit, get you sacked on the spot!'

Gloria's voice had risen to normal levels. More faces turned, eyebrows lifted, lips smiled, frowns wrinkled. The next second she was up, coat wrapped around her with a flick of a hand, lips grazed across my cheeks. Then she was gone. The door flapped shut behind her. And the world went quiet. And monochrome.

I sat, a half-eaten dessert dissolved in front of me, an empty plate with neat lined-up cutlery opposite, and a chair angled by a one-handed push from an exuberant customer who threatened to turn my life on its head. Every day for the next fifty years.

Fourteen

Seven the next evening the buzzer to my door remained silent. My head said 'Told you so' to my heart. At five minutes past seven the buzzer rang. My heart said 'She does things her way' to my head. I quite expected to see Gloria with a suitcase in either hand, a ticket for the railway clutched between her teeth. But she was just sensibly dressed; a light blue swing coat now on the edge of not fashionable, a matched pancake hat perched on fresh-washed hair. Scent of the shampoo haloed her head.

'You're here, I'm here. Seems we got a deal, Roy.'

'Sure does. You still a woman of independent means? Or you lost it all on one of those poker tables you decorate?'

'Huh, I get old fools to do that, I don't risk my own money. And, remember, not till the end of the month. You're my sugar daddy at the moment.'

'In that case the drink'll be sour mighty quick, my salary keeps me in two newspapers a week and two whiskeys at the cheapest bar.'

Gloria hung her arms around my neck, her coat flaps fell open against me, showed off a red check two-piece suit worn underneath. And the buzzer sounded again.

I pulled back from a kiss.

'Heck, you didn't say you had a sister to join us too?'

'One not good enough for you now? I'll have to show you wrong there, won't I?'

Gloria's eyes flashed promises my body quivered at.

'I better get the door, could be Mr Isaacs, second floor, forgot his keys again.'

It wasn't.

The woman stood in the evening gloom dressed practical; short gray coat, dark blue turned up jeans, low-heeled pumps. And a look to kill an army of five thousand. The voice crossed the air in the thickest Apple accent I'd ever heard, and I'd lived every year of my life in the city.

'You must be Dalton. I came for Raccio, I saw her go in minutes ago.'

'And you are...?'

I think I knew the answer before the question flew my mouth.

'Dorothy Galvan. I got a few things to say to Miss Raccio.'

'I'm not sure she...'

Dorothy pushed past, strode into the hallway, looked around, saw my door open, headed in. I floundered after her, an arm extended to haul her back.

'I don't think...'

'So, there you are, you frigging little doxy. Found yourself another guy with brains in his trousers? If you think you're getting a dime from Floyd, you're a frigging fool.'

I came into the room to see Gloria stood face to face with our newcomer. They matched heights; Dorothy probably fought one weight up from her opponent. But then I reckoned Gloria won on experience in back alley brawls. She put hands on her hips like a gunslinger poised to draw fast.

'It's all legal, the lawyer said Floyd had everything written up in triple. I get the apartment, the moolah from the account, our account. You get the rest, the house, the kid, the pension.'

'Over my frigging dead body, Raccio.'

'You got all that, all the other money Floyd and you saved up, whatever. You ain't no pauper out on the sidewalk. Go kiss the lawyer's ass.'

I hovered on the sidelines, unsure whether to intervene. When two dogs stare each other down it can be mighty dangerous to grab one, a mouthful of teeth or a paw of claws can tear your skin to pieces while the antagonists stand unharmed.

Dorothy took a step nearer Gloria. A finger jabbed at the latter's face. The nail looked like it could scar for life.

'You're a dirty call-girl from the trash cans behind the slimiest club in New York. And that's where you end up after a high-rolled Saturday with bennie sellers down Queens. You're not getting a dollar of my son's money.'

Gloria held her stance, held her cool.

'All hot air, Dorothy, you go shout at the lawyer, it'll get you nowhere, everything's typed and signed long ago. Guess Floyd didn't love you as much as you thought, you schnook.'

Floyd's wife moved even nearer, flung an arm at Gloria, the fingers flashed to mark. They met thin air. Gloria swayed back, took no counter action against the flustered woman opposite her.

I decided to remind both I was the guy who rented this fight ring, stepped forward with arms spread wide, palms up and open.

'Hey, ladies, this can't be settled like this. Whatever's took place, we gotta abide by the law, however bad that might seem. Drawing blood here's only gonna get the cops involved, we don't need that.'

Dorothy turned to me.

'Floyd was a frigging cop. They'll beat you senseless if I say you're dirtying his name.'

Gloria beat me to a reply.

'How then they let me go see Floyd in the morgue, late at night when it's closed to the public and family? How come they visit me to see I'm set up right, not drowned in gin at a bar? How come one detective gave me a lift here tonight? They knew about Floyd and me, knew you and him were over, were sided firm with us. Go cuddle your kid, he's worth more than any moolah in the bank.'

The last line had my eyebrows raised. It was a cute sign-off. Dorothy's mouth flapped open, the air and words taken away by the phrase's truth and weight. Her hands stuffed deep into her coat pockets. The danger from sharpened fingernails seemed past.

'You're an asshole, Raccio.'

Dorothy spat on the carpet by Gloria's shoes, took out her right hand from the coat pocket. And pointed a Beretta straight at Gloria's face.

I moved a step back, would have gone further but my back touched the bookcase.

'Jesus, this is crazy. Mrs Galvan...'

The gun remained fixed on Gloria. Dorothy's eyes half-flicked my way.

'Keep out of this, you're just a guy who follows their pants after this sorta broad.'

Gloria hadn't moved, hadn't flinched. I guess she'd faced similar moments in clubs and streets ever since she walked out of school. Maybe she'd even seen guns poked angry around apartment doors when her ma forgot the rent or spent it on gin. She removed her coat slow, dropped it on the sofa, straightened her jacket. All without shifting her eyes from Dorothy. She took a step toward the woman.

'Put the gun back in your pocket, Dorothy. Who's gonna look after your kid if you're sat sorry in jail? Who's gonna wipe his nose and eyes when he's all cried out over losing his pa.'

'I don't care, I want you out the picture, Raccio. I ain't having you living it high on money Floyd earned.'

Gloria inched closer. I could see the movement, I don't think Dorothy did. She was too intent on venting her ire and keeping the Beretta held level. She'd probably never held a weapon before.

'I put a bullet in you, I get it put down to deranged status or whatever, sure a lawyer can get me a short time, maybe none at all. I take out this guy too, I might get away with it all.'

Gloria held her stance. My knees wobbled so weak I near ended up knelt on the carpet. My hand caught the low table in front of me, disturbed a pile of books towered at its middle. Dorothy's eyes glanced my way. Gloria's hand shot out, grabbed the woman's wrist, pulled it down to one side, grasped the same wrist with her other hand to get a firm hold, snapped the held arm over her knee. I heard something crack. Dorothy yelped. Her gun dropped to the carpet. Gloria held the arm one-handed, picked up the Beretta and with the skill of a Marines Weapons Officer flicked out the bullets and let them cascade with a volley of clicks to the floor.

The weapon snapped shut, she held it out to Dorothy, now bent over clutched at her injured wrist.

'I warned you, use it or put it away. Now stuff it somewhere the sun don't shine, or I'll put it there myself. Then vamoose out before I call a cop who worships my ass, puts you against a wall and stuffs his hands where you don't want them.'

Dorothy looked up at Gloria, her make-up melted by tears, part emotion, part pain, I guessed. Then she turned, staggered to the door, pulled it open and disappeared out the building.

Gloria looked down at the gun she still held.

'Darn it, I'll have to stick this in a river, in case it's plugged a guy or two in another life. You breathing, Roy? You look bad.'

I glanced up from my bent over position, hands on my knees, let out a long, slow sigh of relief. My whole life, desperately short and dull, had flashed before me. I'd been sure Dorothy was going to shoot.

Gloria walked over, the Beretta hung loose from her fingers.

'C'mon, I wanna get this baby in deep water, in case that broad runs into a cop stood lazy on a street corner and cries out a tale of heartbreak with a promise of a dirty cuddle in bed tonight.'

'Sure, sure, you lead, I'll follow, lock up behind us.'

Gloria picked up her coat, swung it on, tucked the gun into a pocket.

'After, we come back here? I can stay the night? Guess you might go nuts by yourself. You ain't used to this kinda stuff.'

'Yeah, sure, anything. Let's go, get back. Grab a take out on the way?'

'Hey, you're better already, thinking of his stomach, that's my guy.'

'No, but I need something to stop the shakes, and I don't wanna start on whiskey.'

Gloria slapped me hard on a shoulder.

'Gee, Roy, I'm gonna have to harden you up if you're gonna run my outfit this side of the city.'

'What...?'

A smile spread over Gloria's face. She stepped back to guffaw, turned away, then back.

'I'm pulling those weak-shook legs of yours, I ain't going anywhere near bad stuff now, I got legit money, haven't I? I set up a club, it's gonna be run by the laws.'

'Glad to hear that. But you wanna run a club, after all you been through in them?'

'No, just came into my little old head. C'mon, the river first, then we walk to a diner, plan whether we stay in the Apple or go chase a sunset out west.'

It was dark on the sidewalk, drizzle hung in the air, like a jury undecided over our future plans. We locked arms, walked like a regular couple. Except for the gun weighted down in Gloria's pocket. She leaned across, kissed my cheek.

'Whatever happens, Roy, promise you'll always be my stranger to love. Never change from that.'

She reached over, kissed my cheek a second time.

'I promise. Got a feeling being with you is gonna be a strange ride anyway.'

Gloria's face lit up the street, dulled every light for a hundred yards, paled the Moon to insignificance.

'Strange is beautiful, Roy, you'll see.'

Fifteen

We planned to meet the next day at my apartment. After a meal my nerves had straightened out so we decided to split up; Gloria went to let the gun kiss water, I collapsed on my bed, dreamt dreams mixed with horror and bliss.

Gloria had days to wait until the legal sentences were typed up with every period finalized. I had work I didn't want to pull out of, needed time to decide how I could move to another city, continue my training. And where were we headed to? It was one thing to state out loud in euphoria late at night, highed in love, we were leaving town. But it was something else to decide where, and how, and when. The cold light of day and all that.

I sat hunched over my desk, the hubbub of office life drifted ignored around me. Words focused for minutes, blurred for tens of minutes. My short greetings earlier no doubt raised looks among the secretaries and juniors. To act natural when your life is half-turned to upside down is easy, if you earn your dollars in front of cameras with directors yelled hoarse shouting 'Cut. Go again, you dolt!'. My eyes flicked to the large clock hung angled on the front wall. It drummed out time like one of those beefed up guys on a Roman galley who kept the slaves rowed in time.

I managed to hit a few minutes with words read sensible in my head. Until a hand smacked hard on my shoulder. Dan grinned at my side, leaned low over the table, a newspaper clutched in one hand.

'Hey, thought you'd have the early edition spread over your work.'

'Why? What's it about you and being the first to read the damn papers every day?'

I looked up, eyes blinked to focus on Dan's smile-creased face. He shook his head.

'Here, leave that legal garbage. This is the real world, in every dirty detail.'

Dan flourished the newspaper over my files. It flirted with dipping its corner in my cooled coffee. He flicked the pages over to an inside section. A finger stabbed at a poor-quality photograph which showed two city policemen stood peered down at something huddled on the sidewalk. Neon lights illuminated a store front, told me we were in a less than salubrious part of town.

'So? Another night in New York, another call out for the boys?'

'A broad. Gunned down on the sidewalk. Bullets sprayed everywhere. Bar one, caught her through the throat, bled her out quick.'

'And? Like I said, another night, another piece of paper for the boys to fill in before they go for beers.'

'My contact reckons the shooter was an amateur, the shots smacked a wall all over, five bullets in brickwork and glass, only one on target. Or, and get this, they might've been using their wrong arm. Possibly got an injury or maybe a gunshot wound in their regular one. Kinda crazy, don't you think?'

My eyes had begun to sharpen on the words peeped out from Dan's newspaper. He came in near every day with a story found in print. Most ran out of steam after two sentences of dialog. But this time his words nagged my head.

'Wrong arm? They got a name?'

'Who for?'

'Either. The shooter. Or the victim.'

'Er, let's see, I didn't look see that. Yeah, got a name here.'

Dan's finger traced down to the final paragraph of the report.

'Yeah, see, 'The precinct can't confirm identification at this stage, but sources suggest the victim is believed to be one Gloria Raccio, a known hostess in clubs owned by the notorious Cigar Charlie'.'

My body froze. My lungs froze. My heart froze. The pen in my fingers blotted a footnote I'd just added. Dan dragged his finger off the newspaper.

'Hey, that's the broad we saw a few times in that poker place. Wasn't she the one you had your eye on at one stage? Told you she was trouble. And in trouble. Reckon a played-out poker player wanted his moolah back, or a wife got angry over Gloria's hand wandering wayward over her husband's body.'

I tried to breathe. A lump stuck in my throat. I stood up quick, rumpled up the newspaper with one hand, sent my documents sliding over the edge of the table into a slow cascade onto the floor. I turned toward Dan, couldn't go face-to-face with him, kept my eyes on the disturbed table.

'I need this.'

'Sure, I...'

I was out the door before Dan could finish his sentence, the eyes of the secretaries half-lifted toward me, fingers still fast-typed in front of them. The air outside, fresh in the early morned city, startled me, my feet stumbled on steps I walked up and down daily. I reached out, caught the railing by their side with one hand, steadied myself, folded the newspaper up crooked. Quick paces took me toward the park, somewhere to be alone.

The bench was cold, damp from the night before. I spread the paper over my lap, reread the report. My heart heaved, broke, stayed broke.

I fumbled inside my jacket, drew out an envelope. The brown paper ripped easy in my fingers, the white sheet inside ripped in unison. I dropped the pieces on the path in front of me. A life represented by a dozen torn shreds, drifted around by a breeze, soaking up wetness from concrete. My resignation, written in the virgin hours of this once optimistic morning.

Printed in Great Britain
by Amazon